MOSS

by

Jane Palmer

To Sarah,
With Best Wishes,

Jane

19.8.14

DODO BOOKS

First published in Great Britain
by Dodo Books 2014

This is a work of fiction and any
resemblance to persons living or dead is
purely coincidental.

The author asserts the moral right to be identified as
the author of this work.

ISBN 978 1 906442 33 0

Chapter 1

From her study in the large cupola surmounting Fairdamon's library, Ko Tricali watched the farmers carrying boxes of soft fruit to preserve for the winter. The glass canopy that protected the apricots, strawberries and tomatoes caught the sun and gleamed like ruby in its setting rays. Soon the apples would be ripe enough to store and root vegetables ready to earth up. Whatever the season, Fairdamon never went without carrots and parsnips while the rest of the country starved. The Fairdamons might have felt guilt over that, but people outside their walled town depended on animal husbandry for their diet and, as with heretics, regarded vegetarians as aberrations.

Her assistant's expectant expression as he anticipated each new revelation to issue from the tip of her quill was disconcerting, so Ko Tricali laid it aside and sent him to bring refreshments.

Some of the manuscripts they worked on were old transcriptions from an earlier language even Ko, with all her expertise, could not decipher. And then there were the fragments of ancient text on linen, wood and papyrus. Assembling them into a sensible order had taken the librarian and her staff years.

Ko took a deep, resigned breath, and adjusted her eyeglasses - one of the few useful things that had come from outside the isolated town of Fairdamon. Otherwise the medicines her people used were so in advance of those possessed by the world they shunned, their doctors would have been accused of witchcraft had they left the town's walls to treat the victims of plague now raging across the country. Fairdamons were already regarded as interlopers from an ancient pagan cult, and attempting to help their benighted, puritanical neighbours would not only have been futile, but dangerous.

So there the community was compelled to stay,

behind the high walls, living in relative comfort, eating their own produce and contemplating the hugeness of an unknowable Universe. They had all the time in the world to try and make sense of how their ancestors had walked the planet like beneficent daemons, educating the very people who would now have them hanged as witches.

On the desk before Ko was the earliest known papyrus fragment, the one all translators came back to in an attempt to tease another small gem from its disjointed script.

"In those days lived giants..."

After that a tantalising amount of text was missing until, "Lands were fertile," then a much argued over inflection, "The people prospered...." or was it, "The giants helped people prosper."?

Ko took the beverage her assistant had made them and silently contemplated the unknowable origins of her giants, who not only pre-dated the people they knew, but probably several ice ages as well. At least the librarians had pieced together enough to document the extraordinary lives of ancestors who became legends to the primitive tribes they had helped to survive. Their benevolent sensibilities had not been emulated and those "golden giants" remained long enough to wonder what sort of creatures they had helped to plunder their beloved world.

It was not in the philosophy of the Fairdamons to harbour regrets, yet they knew that the best intentions could have unfortunate consequences. Ko could only hope that at some time in the future these people would become more aware and less self-obsessed. Then, perhaps, the truth could be told.

The irony was, if it had not been for an outsider - and one from a religious order at that - even these ancient texts would have been lost. Brother Petrus had been a remarkable man and his historical accounts were much easier to read, being only in mediaeval Latin. The mere fact that he risked committing his encounter with the Fairdamons to a chronicle spoke volumes about the monk's courage and veracity. Had his writing fallen into the wrong hands, he would have certainly been condemned as a heretic.

Chapter 2

The sun was trying to rise milkily through the early spring mist.

Black-booted men were surreptitiously loading weapons from a lock-up garage into the back of some lorries. It was too early in the morning for the local residents to be bothered about the manoeuvres of the sinister brigade in fascist tunics. Many districts had them. It was only now that the government warned that Mr Mosley and his jackbooted followers, entertaining the population with their goose-stepping antics long after the Third Reich realised how hard its was on the Achilles tendons, were not harmless eccentrics after all. It was no longer possible to make jokes about what was happening in Europe. Many preferred not to believe it, while realists were aware that the huge, malign cloud sweeping across the continent towards them would not be turned back by wishful thinking.

While the Blackshirts loaded their weapons in the dingy backstreet, a member of the well-heeled gentry was saying goodbye to his family outside their palatial residence, soon to be turned into a dormitory for young people taking refuge from his fascist master's carpet bombing. However much those inner-city children managed to cause havoc, it would be nothing compared to the devastation visited on the neighbourhoods they came from.

The wealth of Penelope Freeman's family came from banking, so their country estate had no need to maintain arable land or sitting tenants. The Georgian manor's facade was elegant, restrained and free of vines, climbing roses, or swastikas. The family butler had made it clear, at whatever the cost, he would report Michael Freeman to the authorities if so much as a thumbnail of Nazi iconography defaced the home of his wife's late, revered parents. It was no doubt fear of Penelope discovering his treacherous affiliations that restrained Freeman. For all the years he had been living there, inheriting its staff as well as the property, he had never been able to take the measure of the mysterious butler, and wasn't prepared to challenge him over so much as a tarnished teaspoon.

The Freeman's family manor house would have been idyllic if it were not for the dubious politics frequently discussed behind its walls. The embroidered Queen Anne chairs had supported the angular rumps of Third Reich sympathisers, and the Victorian sofas the more ample backsides of German (and English) aristocracy who were so detached from reality that surrendering the world to a master race seemed quite rational.

Penelope Freeman remained innocent of what was going on. Never asked to join in their discussions, she was persuaded that her husband's German speaking guests were too civil to be engaged in anything as impolite as the Third Reich. A gardener with an East End accent would have raised more suspicion, which was probably why - apart from her inheritance - Michael Freeman went to such lengths to ensure she became his wife. The cook, butler, maid and gardeners, all aware of what was going on, knew their places. Destroying their gracious mistress's view of a benign universe was not in their terms of contract, so everyone continued to potter about, attending to the tasks that enabled the huge house to run smoothly as though oblivious of the maelstrom already engulfing Europe. There were cordons of peaches to train, a large, lopsided wolfhound to feed, an older brother to be rescued from a precocious infant with destructive tendencies, and gravel to rake over the incriminating

4

tyre tracks of the motorcade that brought their dubious guests.

All the staff could do was breathe a sigh of relief when the master of the house left on his secret jaunt to generate treasonous mischief.

Michael Freeman was good-looking and in his early forties; if there was not something sinister about the man, anyone else meeting him casually might have detected an element of the Latin gigolo. His infatuated wife saw none of these things; he and their two children were her sole reason for existence. Their eight-year-old son hardly resembled his father and lacked any familial force of character. His four-year-old sister had enough for both of them, a little too much for a child barely able to read. No reassuring children's storybooks for her, she would soon be breaking her intellectual teeth on medical non-fiction with all the gruesome details that entailed. This precocious sibling was determined to be a doctor; her placid brother learning to put up with the bandages and poultices for the sake of peace and quiet.

As their father stowed a suitcase in the back of his open top saloon car, family matters were not uppermost in his mind. Penelope Freeman would have asked about the voyage he was about to undertake if the devotion that blinded her had not suppressed the question, in the same way she had always accepted that the guests they so lavishly entertained in their country seat were business associates. In a rare moment of suspicion, the lady of the house had once wondered who they really were but, as her husband had invited them, how could there have been anything wrong about their presence? How could these elegant, polite visitors have been connected with the terrible rumours that were leaking from Europe? The formidable family butler's expression may have hardened at their approach, but the local hunt's dogs liked them, though it was the only time the wolf hound would seek out the protection of its infant tormentor.

5

As her husband drove off into the mist, Penelope Freeman was apprehensive; taking a voyage given the international situation was risky. War could be declared at any moment. Had she been aware that he was meeting up with a gang of Blackshirts armed to the teeth, Michael Freeman's wife might have recalled her cousin's advice about marrying the man in the first place. An amazingly astute woman, Bethany was now cruising the mighty rivers of the Amazon in the search for exotic plants. Penelope would have also been interested in botany had she not at heart been a hausfrau and dedicated hostess to her husband's sophisticated, strange, friends.

Under a leaden sky, Freeman's saloon car rendezvoused with several kaki-covered lorries waiting by the common in Greenbridge village. The only ones disturbed by their presence were the ducks in the pond. Other residents accepted it as a necessary intrusion by an army preparing for invasion, though why Hitler would have needed to invade a small village in the middle of nowhere escaped them. And why the commander of a British army unit would turn up in smart civvies and an expensive saloon car to take his men on manoeuvres was also not something open to question. There must have been a good reason, but that was probably a state secret as well.

As though anticipating the convoy's murky venture, the mist resolutely refused to lift and bless it with a little sunlight. It was well away by the time the morning queue formed outside the local baker.

The khaki lorries droned on behind the open topped saloon car like noisy, obedient caterpillars trying to pursue a butterfly. As they wended their way through narrow lanes, the saloon's paintwork was assailed by brambles more used to ensnaring the flanks of horses and shins of cyclists.

A mile from Greenbridge the road forked into two overgrown routes without a signpost as though the

6

resident troll refused to allow anything larger than a push bike through. But their leader had committed the route to memory and this convoy feared nothing. It was well-armed and prepared to take on the hordes laying siege to Valhalla without so much as disturbing the partings in its combatants greased down hair.

As the saloon crested the brow of a hill, Michael Freeman anticipated the small, ghostly town hiding in the valley, confident that it was not expecting him.

But he was wrong.

A lookout in Fairdamon's tallest Italianate tower had spotted the dull, dung coloured vehicles following the saloon car and quickly wended his way down to announce their arrival.

Chapter 3

Shafts of sunlight from the high windows of the main debating chamber spotlighted a gathering of elders, and other Fairdamons credited with enough common sense to make decisions tempered by the pragmatism of self-preservation. This had always been an egalitarian town where even the innocence of children was heeded. Not on this occasion, however.

Many wore ancient robes for the occasion, as though knowing that this would be the last time they ever saw the light of day. Centuries old, the material still glinted with threads of silver, platinum and gold in the decaying splendour of the ornate chamber. The residents of Fairdamon had at last accepted that the rest of the world was aware of their isolated community. Once human beings had acquired the combustion engine, it was inevitable that their solitude would be disturbed; it was just surprising that it had taken so many decades.

Nor Nagada, the eldest present, was still astute, and determined that some vestige of their glorious past should be preserved when their ancient lineage at last petered out like a guttering, exotic candle. She advised that the young, infirm and elderly be taken to safety on the outskirts of the town.

A burly man, not quite so golden-haired and tall as the others, entered carrying a large bunch of keys.

'Bring up the reality switch, Anthony, and then ensure that the cellar is sealed,' Nor Nagada asked.

Anthony left with three others to descend the steps spiralling round a platform lift shaft and down into a cavern excavated by an underground river, which now trickled along its original massive course as though in apology. The walls of rock were illuminated as they descended, bringing into sharp relief surreal sculptures entwining the towering pillars supporting its roof.

Several recesses above the water line were secured by solid wooden doors and massive locks. Anthony ascended a ramp to the furthest of these and used the keys to turn its many tumblers in strict sequence.

As soon as the door was pulled open lamps inside came on like flickering fridge lights to reveal a jumble of gleaming artefacts never destined to meet the trowel of amateur archaeologist or metal detector. Entombed so deep, behind impenetrable bolts, this ancient hoard was more likely to end up being subducted by continental plate movements before astounding the archaeological dogma of a society that believed it knew everything. Fairdamon's policy had been to allow humankind to go on conjecturing that it was the pinnacle of the planet's intelligent evolution. This fragile glassware pearlised by millennia of storage, and amber bowls that could have only been chased by an advanced technology, would never be seen by those more inclined to drill the ocean for oil than gaze at the stars for enlightenment.

But precious tableware was not what the keyholder and his companions had come down for. Tucked away amongst the treasure, almost in embarrassment, was a large, dull box crouching like a toad in the waterlilies.

It took all four men to lift it out and manoeuvre it onto the platform lift where it was carried up to see daylight for the first time in centuries.

Chapter 4

When Michael Freeman reached Fairdamon he realised that the only way in for his convoy was through the ornamental gates in its high, stone wall that would have kept out a tank.

While the vehicles waited in the narrow road circling the ancient town he calculated how much explosive would be needed to blow out the pillars supporting the gates' heavy hinges.

Before the order could be given the gates slowly opened as though sensing his expertise with dynamite.

There was no one about. It had to be a trap. The faces of the mythological wrought iron beasts gazing down with alien expressions would have daunted any other visitors. But these invaders had a mission, a keen sense of the mystical and were heavily armed. They were confident their destiny lay in their Aryan descent and heavenly crystal spheres from which they originated.

Michael Freeman's saloon car cautiously led the other vehicles down a winding road into the small town of Fairdamon. Its cupolas, towers, and decorative ridges caught the morning sun's rays as the mist at last lifted, setting the stage for a bizarre drama even he could not have anticipated.

The architecture was not what he had been expecting. It should have been more monumental, like the work of Albert Speer, not a politely decaying Portmeirion. Fairyland turrets and towers jutted up through the lingering mist from steeply gabled roofs, and terraced houses clung magically to the valley walls. The town should have had that robust Bavarian elegance in its architecture; this was more like a

Romanesque cake iced with white marble and sprinkled with small, glinting windmills and screens to collect the rays of the rising sun.

The convoy drove on to the town's large square surrounded by a colonnade. A tall woman, as ancient and mysterious as her surroundings, stood at its centre.

As Freeman left his saloon car, an inexplicable sensation of finality invaded his mind. He shuddered. But the German agent was made of stern stuff and pushed the intrusive thought aside. He strode over to confront the imposing woman. Her strands of glinting silver hair played in the light thermals channelled through the narrow streets radiating away from the square. Nor Nagada could have been anything between seventy and 700. Her tall, straight stance had never known bone loss and that stern gaze could have stopped a tiger in its tracks. The ankle length robe she wore was also ancient and studded with a rainbow of unfamiliar gems. If Fairdamon was an enchanted town, this woman was its supreme wizard because she seemed to know why he was there.

She continued to gaze steadily at the intruder without blinking or bothering to glance at the heavily armed men climbing from the backs of the lorries.

'We knew somebody would eventually come,' Nor Nagada eventually announced. 'We just did not expect it would be on behalf of Adolf Hitler.'

As an Abwher agent, Freeman prided himself on not allowing his movements to be known by anyone, let alone that he was a German spy. 'How can you know who we are?'

'The rumour of Fairdamon possessing the ultimate weapon has been absorbed into local mythology. Unlike most who believe it to be a myth, only someone committed to the evil absurdity of Nazi superiority would pursue the rumour as fact.'

The intruder squinted in annoyance at her distain for his crusade to install a Teutonic hell on Earth: at least, that seemed to be what this unworldly, uncompromising hag was suggesting. Despite that, there could be no doubting that she came from Aryan stock. Her silver hair still sparkled with golden strands and the tall, straight limbed posture verged on the Valkyrie. Yet the woman stood before him, radiating contempt so fiercely the armed men behind him must have been aware of it.

Her defiance could have only meant one thing.

'Who else knows we are here?'

'The war machine in this country is driven by more rational considerations, like self preservation and trying not to release their tenuous grip on an empire. They do not believe that there is such a doomsday machine because they dare not. Only those who truly hold life so cheap would not flinch from using it.'

'Then it does exist?'

'Of course.'

It had to be a trap, yet Freeman was unable to fathom how.

'Well, don't you want it then?' There was a challenge in the elderly woman's tone.

He hardly dare believe his ears. 'What?'

'It is of no use to us. We do not intend to take over the world.'

'If you believe I'm an enemy agent, why are you willing to let me have such a dangerous weapon?'

'It is of no consequence to us who uses it. Each side will annihilate the other soon enough. There are levels of reality no human can comprehend, and whatever happens here will make little difference to them.'

'Our reality is the only reality!' stormed Freeman.

'So why you are willing to destroy it?'

'Your weapon will be well used by the master race.'

Nor Nagada gave him a pitying look before beckoning four men standing in the colonnade to bring over a large, bland box. The Aryan in Freeman could only admire the tall, golden-haired Fairdamons, their muscles straining under the weight of the doomsday machine. Could these men be descended from a branch of the master race that his paymasters were unaware of? He wasn't going to find out; the old woman waved them away. They hesitated, so she pointed firmly to one of the streets radiating from the square. They obeyed her command and reluctantly left. Now he had the weapon - whatever it was - within his reach and without a fight.

'How do you activate the device,' Freeman demanded.

Nor Nagada gave a mysterious smile and took a small crystal rod from her gown pocket. This she inserted into a slot in the lid and then, with unconcerned deftness, dialled a code into the panel beside it as though about to book a reservation at the Ritz.

The heavy lid slowly lifted.

A dazzling light virtually howled from cavernous depths as the entity in the box woke.

Freeman's men stepped back and aimed their guns at the device.

'There is no need to be alarmed. What did you expect from the most powerful weapon ever created?'

Freeman also hadn't expected to find himself peering down the throat of an enraged dragon.

The lid slowly yawned wider to reveal another control panel, though the light was too intense for him to see the core of the device.

It took all of Freeman's willpower to avoid showing that he was astounded. 'What is it?'

'Your means to conquer the world - or destroy it.'

'How does it work?' he demanded.

'It is necessary to dial the correct sequence to release the safety locks.'

'Show me how it's done.'

She gazed at him long and hard. 'You wish me to activate it?'

'Just show me how it works,' Freeman demanded.

'No, you do not believe our reality to merely be the

tip of a cosmic dimension beyond human comprehension, do you?'

How dare this ancient hag sneer at his superiority! 'So prove me wrong, woman, and let this machine reveal the face of God!' Freeman ordered, confident that she would not do it.

Nor Nagada smiled icily and dialled in another code. The panel flashed out a complex sequence as she unlocked each safety protocol. Blue and violet lights chased each other faster and faster until the panel became a dazzling blur.

Freeman's men drew closer. Although daunted, their curiosity was ensnared by the astonishing machine. How could such a wonderful device be the harbinger of death?

Yet it was.

Too late, Freeman realised what was happening. 'Switch it off! Switch it off!' he screamed.

The old woman raised her hands. 'Prepare to be enlightened.'

An innocent sounding "click" issued from the depths of the box.

A globe of plasma roared from it and engulfed everyone, giving them just enough time to see the flesh fall from the amazed faces of the others.

The horror remained soundless as the Fairdamon stood, hands raised, until she dissolved into the fierce furnace of energy.

Reality stuttered and guttered out for everyone. The men's tissue became a sticky smog that coated the colonnade and cloisters behind them.

Then followed the explosion that shook every parish for twenty miles.

Chapter 5

Greenbridge Village had only just accepted the miracle of electric street lighting. Many of its residents refused to trust this new source of energy, still cooking with gas and reading by oil lamps; crystal sets were for people who had nothing better to do, and the threatened advent of television was an intrusion to be warded off with bell, book and candle.

It had also taken the villagers centuries to accept their sophisticated neighbours in Fairdamon, during which time they had spread rumours about their extraordinary satanic powers. Their malnourished ancestors had resented the unholy way these people towered over them like angels of an impending apocalypse. No one in Greenbridge had actually expected the Fairdamons to bring about the end of the world of course, except a succession of vicars who regularly had the Church boundaries reconsecrated as a precaution, so they were somewhat taken aback when it did apparently arrive.

The village watched, dumbfounded, as a dome of livid orange, shot through with lightning, engulfed Fairdamon. The pulsating cloud ballooned into the sky where it rotated like an angrily shaken eiderdown in the stratosphere, threatening to rain malice.

All the rumours local wisdom had dismissed as fable about that forbidden, secretive town were now confirmed. Only the doomsday weapon of legend could have generated such a maelstrom in the atmosphere, not unless war had been declared without their knowledge and Hitler possessed technology beyond their scientists.

PC Knowles dashed from the barber shop, moustache half-trimmed and chin lathered in shaving foam. While the rest of the village stood and stared at the furious sky, the local bobby dashed back inside to use the barber's telephone, wiped away the foam, tossed on his helmet, and jumped on his bike which he had leaned against the pole outside.

PC Knowles was pink, portly and bewhiskered, a 45-year-old man who could have been taken for 60. The magnificent moustache that he had regularly trimmed would have looked splendid on a fakir, and rumour claimed that his grandfather had indeed been a sepoy in the Indian Raj. Friendly and fair, he was the ideal pillar of strength that no salacious gossip could defame with its venom. Even the local squire would doff his hat as PC Knowles and his comely wife walked up the high street, and not only because she was one of the few women to repel his advances. He knew about her husband's courage under fire and gave the man respect when most other locals deserved the taste of his riding crop.

Shouting to everyone to get inside as he went, the stalwart upholder of the law peddled furiously towards Fairdamon. Nobody paid attention - few ever did - but they admired the man all the same; he had to be riding into certain death.

A young mother, child in arms, demanded to know why the able-bodied men of the village were not accompanying PC Knowles. Only then did the adult male population take his advice and make themselves scarce.

'Leave them be,' the postmistress called from her shop door. 'There's no reason why anyone here should risk their lives for people who choose to live behind a high wall.'

'Then phone the Home Office - or someone... Mr Knowles couldn't have had time to tell anyone what's really happening.' Then the young woman dashed home for fear of what the sinister sky was liable to shower down on the children she had left playing in the garden.

As the glowing cloud expanded and rose higher, bolder villagers who hadn't taken cover started to hold hushed, fearful conversations about the unknown power of Nazi armaments, or the evil that had permeated the region since the dawn of time. They concluded that this catastrophe could not have been caused by mere mortals. It took an older, wiser resident to remind them that Fairdamon had never done any harm and only brought Greenbridge prosperity. If the town had been destroyed, who would buy their sundry goods and farm produce which the walled town was unable to grow for itself with its dwindling population? Yet it did somehow seem inevitable that their mysterious neighbours would eventually disappear without explanation in a splendid cataclysm, leaving only rumour and conjecture.

The old resident was right. Something astounding and unfathomable had passed and the Fairdamons would be missed.

The sinister cloud slowly dissipated into the upper atmosphere where it made pearlised scrolls against the cobalt sky.

When PC Knowles reached Fairdamon its gates were standing wide open for the first time he could remember, framing the valley filled with eddies of smoke and dust.

The constable cycled down as far as he could before dismounting to clamber over the rubble blocking the road to the square. Every fibre of commonsense told him to wait. Unfortunately for PC Knowles, his sense of responsibility overrode it. What if there were survivors needing assistance, or risk of further explosions which could devastate the whole region?

The flagstones of the square had been turned to glass, creating a mirror like pavement. At its centre was a crater so large it could have hidden two dozen double-decker buses. All that remained was the colonnade, its broken pillars like so many jagged teeth around Hell's portal.

It took the constable some while to comprehend the enormity of the incident.

And then he noticed the human fragments. After a career of only having to deal with the odd black eye and bruised dignity, the memory of his nightmare months in the trenches returned. It was just as sickening now to stumble across an incinerated arm or part of a head. Having found the remains of one body, the constable went on to identify others; some consumed in the conflagration, others nothing but stains on the vitrified ground.

By the time a police car arrived in Greenbridge, the pall of a smoke lingering over Fairdamon was just a haze in the upper atmosphere. When they reached the town PC Knowles had collapsed on the glassy ground amongst the body parts. As soon as it arrived, he was hurried to the Red Cross van accompanying the troops who were rapidly deployed to search for survivors.

Only then did Fairdamon's small population warily emerge from hiding. They approached the invasion of dark blue and khaki uniforms as though encountering another lifeform for the first time. These golden-haired people were much taller than their highest ranking officer in attendance, and intrigued the military and police personnel with their calm, detached bearing.

Little was learnt from the Fairdamons, not even why they had luggage as though knowing that they would have to at last emerge from the cloistered safety of their town.

However mysterious, it seemed unlikely that these people could have possessed a weapon capable of determining the outcome of the looming war. Despite this, every man, woman and child fell under suspicion. Not one of them was ever allowed to escape authority's attention again. After centuries of isolation, they would become the country's closest guarded secret watched by the same authorities that had apparently overlooked the treasonable activities of Michael Freeman.

It was eventually decided that the Fairdamons' tall, elegant appearance was due to inbreeding and not Aryan descent, yet it damned them all the same. While a treacherous-hearted mole had been able blend in so well and walk the British streets, these golden geese could only strut the lawns behind barbed wire... Apart from one young couple.

Clutching a child and the keys to Fairdamon's subterranean vault, they had left the walled town through a secret gate. Even though the detonation of the reality switch must have blocked the steps down to Fairdamon's treasure hoard, and possibly demolished the cave's roof, those keys could not fall into the wrong hands. These two young adults were the fittest of an ailing population and best suited to survive in a hostile world, long enough to prevent their people's ancient secrets falling into avaricious human hands. Allana Olandas was also one of the few in the town able to drive the motorbike locked away in a stone bunker outside the wall for just such an emergency. With Norbas Oradonte, her husband, and Johab their son, safely stowed in the sidecar, she kicked the machine into life.

The family was well away before it had occurred to the military that there might have been another way out of the walled town. They were more focused on the cataclysmic explosion. Not even the munitions used in the Great War could have vitrified stone and vaporised bodies in such a manner.

When it also became apparent that PC Knowles was suffering from something far more serious than shock, the town was quarantined and its population evacuated to remote, unoccupied army barracks. The Fairdamons went without complaint, as though knowing a cosmic secret that made it worth putting up with the indignity.

Then the strange people who had been isolated for so long rapidly started to die of a pneumonic condition that confounded a hard-pressed medical profession. They attributed it to pathogens in the dust cloud created by the explosion which had destroyed the centre of their town.

PC Knowles didn't survive the night.

After the autopsy, the local undertaker tidied up the local hero's rudely interrupted shave and the village gave him a grand funeral to cover their guilty relief that they hadn't accompanied their late, lamented constable.

Chapter 6

The hard-featured General Doncaster glared at the line of camp beds as though the seriously ill subalterns laying on them had been guilty of insubordination.

He jabbed an accusing finger at one of the unfortunate soldiers, 'If that man is only nineteen his hair shouldn't be falling out like that.'

The MI5 agent accompanying him shrugged. 'Same thing happened to the others who didn't survive.'

'Why wasn't I told sooner?'

'That was a police decision. Officer-in-charge thought it was a civil matter until Major Judd turned up and assumed control.'

'How could the man have thought a thundering great explosion like that was caused by civilians?'

'It's a pity the civilians living here won't tell us.'

'This has cost God knows how many lives.'

'I just hope no stupid arse in the Home Office decides to give Michael Freeman a commendation.'

General Doncaster cast his iron glare at the dishevelled agent who hadn't slept for 36 hours. 'So what really happened?'

'Freeman was an Abwher spy. Barely anything of him left, but we found documents in what remained of his saloon car confirming he was here.'

'Good God man! Mosley can't have anything this powerful!'

'We doubt it. He's watched too closely and his blackshirts don't have the scientific intelligence to produce so much as a damp squib.'

'Why didn't you have someone watching Freeman?'

'Our informer thought that he was boarding a ship bound for Ireland. We didn't even know that this place existed.'

'Then Heaven help us when Adolf does decide to invade.'

Penelope Freeman received the news that her husband was missing with dignified grace.

Her 11-year-old son, Fred, had never liked his father very much so said nothing. Her four-year-old daughter, Lottie, threw a tantrum and broke a few toys. She wasn't quite sure why, but it usually had the desired effect of making other people keep away from her. She was too young to have emotional issues about her intensely handsome, distant father; just knowing he would no longer be coming back with Belgium chocolates or an Austrian musical box had imprinted on her adolescent mind and would lurk there for the rest of her life. The beauty of being considered an infant was that no one accused you of having hypocritical, adult sentiments.

The family never did discover what had really happened to Michael Freeman. They wondered, yet his widow somehow knew that the matter should not be pursued. As the country was on the verge of war, she secretly feared finding out some horrible revelation her faithful family butler was apparently going to great lengths to cushion her from. He was all too aware that if the truth about Michael Freeman was made public, her home and fortune would have been confiscated as the property of a traitor, committing the family to a penury they would not know how to cope with.

Mr Chapman, their solicitor, also suspected that Michael Freeman's affiliations had more to do with the Third Reich than East European business matters. He assumed that he was now in Germany calling "Heil Hitler" at the ludicrous rallies Busby Berkeley might well have better choreographed had he put symmetry before entertainment. Penelope Freeman was an honourable, not very perceptive, woman who deserved better. Had Lottie been 20 years older she would have been quite capable of supporting her guileless mother and dilatory brother but, being only four, she needed to throw a few more tantrums before setting about an unsuspecting world. At least Mr Chapman could guide Fred towards some useful occupation against his natural inclination to just watch the world go by. That boy needed a forceful woman to guide him once he came of age, which could prove a little trickier.

Penelope Freeman was soon distracted from her loss by several evacuees who taught her oldest offspring more about life than his years spent in the village school with the children of local farmers who could count sheep but not spell "cow". Lottie revelled in the intrigues, squabbles and misdemeanours introduced from the East End. It was only the vigilant butler who saved the young guests from being punished by the intimidating housekeeper hired to keep them in order, for the criminal acts she engineered. Fred kept away from it all and spent his free time playing chess with a young Dutch evacuee who spoke three languages and could identify every element in the periodic table. She was a little scary, but the sort of girl he yearned to marry, if only as a defence against his chaotically maturing sister.

Having survived the War, briefly fostering one of the evacuees (unfortunately not the chess player) who had lost his family, and rationing, Penelope Freeman was surprised that she had managed so well without her husband. Now, when she told Lottie to behave, her daughter, mostly, listened.

As Mr Chapman had anticipated, Lottie was the one who went on to university to study medicine and become the terror of any man who dared to deride female ability. One well landed left hook nearly got her expelled, at the same time bringing her the respect reasoned debate with dull minds could not. One paramour was courageous enough to actually marry Lottie, but died young. Fred was the only one not to wonder why after he had been caught philandering once too often. His principal concern was in keeping the eventful life of Lottie from their mother who now assumed her daughter to be a paragon selflessly ministering to the needs of the sick.

After qualifying, Dr Lottie Freeman became an NHS general practitioner, but also set up her own private surgery, believing that the State should not have to pay for the treatment of the wealthy she was quite capable of ministering to. Fred suspected that she would throw one of her tantrums if told that she was being just as capitalist as everyone else who claimed to be socially aware. At least Lottie Freeman had never been known to make a wrong diagnosis.

Chapter 7

'The Chamber of Dreams was a place where Fairdamons became one with the Universe. It was insulated from every sound and filled with jewels of light that floated from person to person to help dispel intrusive thoughts. Beyond mortal awareness lays a greater, incomprehensible reality, where our humdrum concerns are insignificant. Fairdamons became adept at letting their consciousness float free from their body into this luminous dimension until, one day, nightmare invaded the Chamber of Dreams.'

Moses held his breath. He knew what nightmares were, even though he seldom experienced them in his sheltered existence protected from the brutalities of less fortunate children's lives. He was privileged to have the best of teachers, a knowledgeable mother and older brother. They would go on to explain the Universe once he had the ability to identify the ships that could be seen from his bedroom window, passing against the stars on the far horizon.

As his mother related the story about the Chamber of Dreams, Moses noticed the warmth of her natural fragrance change; something that never happened when she was telling a fanciful fairy tale to lull him to sleep.

Allana Olandas realised that her younger son was listening a little too intently and wondered whether she should continue. His brother had heard the story when he was only four without any ill effects, but through necessity Johab had been a more mature child. Perhaps she had cosseted Moses a little too much. But the story had to be told. There was a glitch in the sensitive Fairdamon mind that allowed in demons. Psychiatrists would have diagnosed the condition as schizophrenia, but these enigmatic people knew that spectres from the dungeons of a universe they endeavoured to comprehend really existed. Even if the demons of their ancestors never troubled Moses, he would need the mental strength to know how to keep secrets from an intrusive world for the rest of his life.

So Allana went on. 'Out of the hallowed silence arose a buzzing sound. At first soft, it increased in volume, permeating the very walls of the Chamber of Dreams and breaking everyone's contemplation. They realised that the sinister noise came from an elemental force which had insinuated itself from its own terrifying dimension into Fairdamon's peaceful refuge. The buzzing intensified. A ghastly phantom appeared. This became engorged on their panic and filled the domed chamber like an evil jellyfish.'

Moses was horrified. 'This didn't really happen, did it mother?'

She smiled benignly. Perhaps he would never be ready. 'Of course not, Moses. There is no such thing as pure evil, and certainly not the sort that can manifest itself.'

'Please go on then.' Moses could deal with an imagined monster. He had seen all the episodes of

Quatermass without looking away because he realised that the horrors in them could never be real.

'Everyone in the Chamber of Dreams barely managed to escape before their minds were invaded by the entity's malevolence.

'The town's council hurriedly gathered and while they debated what to do the monster grew and grew until the walls of the Chamber blazed with heat. It was threatening to crack open its dome and burst out into the unsuspecting world.

The young boy's eyes were wide with horror. 'But where did this creature come from?'

'Thoughts.'

'Thoughts?'

'Blinkered conviction, when strong enough, can raise demons.'

'But whose thoughts?'

'People beyond the walls of Fairdamon were very naive in those days, and this entity might have been a conjured up by the Devil that their Church had taught them to believe in.'

Moses was relieved that it was only a fable after all. 'So the monster was really made of other people's thoughts?'

'The way you perceive the world depends on the thoughts you have. That is why you must guard them carefully. Destructive ones usually only harm the person to have them but, sometimes, when they are many and powerful enough, they can be manifested into something evil.'

'What did the council do?'

'They had no choice but to use the reality switch.'

'What is that?'

'It was a device of such terrible power it could dissolve towns.'

'Like the ones the Americans used to destroy those Japanese cities?'

'That was not its purpose. Our ancestors lived in dangerous times and needed a means to defend

24

themselves, however much it went against their nature. It was such a dreadful device it could only be used as a last resort.'

'What happened to the monster?'

'The reality switch destroyed the Chamber of Dreams and the creature was pushed back into the minds that gave it birth. The explosion was seen in hamlets miles away. This reinforced the conviction outsiders had that Fairdamon was the gateway to Hell. Until then, the town had avoided the attention of the world that surrounded it, the population merely being regarded as heretics. Now Fairdamons also became demons and their priests demanded our persecution.'

'What is a heretic?'

'Anyone who did not worship to their rules.'

'Why didn't they explain why they used the reality switch?'

'And admit to raising the Devil?'

Moses went to bed very puzzled that night. He lay awake gazing at a friendly ducks on his wallpaper, wondering at this unstable thing his people called reality. It was difficult to understand in the warm security he had only known.

Chapter 8

The rising sun's rays cast a rosy sheen over the sea that stretched away to the misty horizon from where, in France, a fog horn could be heard like the mellow voice of a contented cow in a new pasture.

As Moses skipped along the tideline, wondering whether to test the chill water, life was still idyllic. He was now ten and mature enough to realise that nothing stayed the same forever and he should appreciate the good moments while they lasted. His father had been a generous, kind man, but he was long gone. Johab, his older brother, should have been with him, skipping self-consciously along the golden strand, if he had not been ill with the same debilitating illness.

Moses turned to glance at his mother's isolated cottage just visible over the dunes, the last left standing in a road that had been undermined by the sea. Somehow she had encouraged vegetables and flowers to survive the salt breezes and give their home an air of comfortable normality. Another winter storm like the last could wash that away as well, perhaps with them inside it.

Time to pack.

Moses trudged home over the loose sand which filled his sandals.

He stopped before he reached the cottage. A visitor had arrived in a dark car. His mother had mentioned that someone from Land Registry might call to verify her intention about leaving the property to the sea that had swept away its neighbours, and needed confirmation that she was the legal owner.

Moses warily picked his way past the marron grass, sea thrift and yellow poppies to the tidy garden filled with lavender, lobelia and geraniums circled by a picket fence. The sheltered plot at the rear of the cottage was filled with beans, brassicas, soft fruit and root vegetables which Moses would regularly weed. He had known no other home and assumed all children lived in places just as idyllic. It was disconcerting that the real world was about to intrude.

As he opened the front door Moses immediately detected an unpleasant smell of intrigue about the car's owner.

'Shake the sand from your sandals, Moses. When we have gone, the sea can bring in as much as she likes.'

'Yes mother.' Moses removed his sandals and shook the sand from them before stepping inside.

The visitor, wearing a dark blue suit and trilby, acknowledged Moses with a brief incline of the head which was even more worrying than the fact he was carrying a gun. It was well concealed of course, but mother and son were well aware he had it.

'This is Mr Alcott, Moses. It appears that our unusual name is the same as that of another family he is looking for.'

Mr Alcott was one of those anonymous men with a carefully cultivated ambience that smelt bland. Moses wasn't sure why he didn't like him, but knew that his arrival meant trouble. His mother was thinking the same, but was able to conceal her suspicion with elegant confidence. If she hadn't been his mother, Moses would still have admired her. She always looked so perfect in those pastel, floral dresses made from the meagre remnants rationing allowed and, when there was no one else to see, diamonds and pearls that must have been worth a fortune. Perhaps that was why Mr Alcott was here? To take away her jewellery. It was a silly suspicion, but the stranger must never find out about them. There were so many things he must never find out.

Moses knew what he was expected to say. 'Are his family from Wales as well, mother, or perhaps we have Huguenot relatives we know nothing about?'

'It is unlikely Moses. Mr Alcott believes the family he is looking for was born in an English town.'

'What does he think you have done, mother? Robbed a bank or organised a black market ring?'

Mr Alcott looked peevish at the frivolity with which they were treating a matter he obviously regarded of national importance. 'The Land Registry notified us when your name came up in the purchase of a new property, Mrs Oradonte.'

'I believe that the only thing which will persuade Mr Alcott we are who we say we are, Moses, is by showing in him your late father's and my birth certificates. Please fetch the attaché case with the family documents.'

Moses could see the "at last we're getting somewhere" expression cross their visitor's face. 'Of course mother.'

27

'Who do you believe we really are?' she asked firmly as soon as her son had left.

The visitor realised that it was pointless trying to elicit her co-operation without being honest. 'Just before the outbreak of war a community of Nazi collaborators were interned. There was an epidemic and most of them died.'

'How dreadful.' Allana Oradonte seemed to display illogical concern for these confederates of Hitler.

Mr Alcott assumed that this misplaced sympathy was due to the human empathy he lacked. 'Quite.'

'What happened to the survivors?'

There was no point in denying anything now. 'It appears that this serious infection had been latent. They died shortly after the war ended.'

'How does this concern us?'

'One of the families was unaccounted for. We believe the couple's name was either Olandas or Oradonte.'

'I see. So you are here to make sure that we are not these Nazi sympathisers?'

'Something like that.'

'Surely, as the war has been over for several years, this hardly matters any more? Or were they guilty of war crimes?'

Mr Alcott looked uncomfortable. 'It relates to another matter I am not at liberty to discuss.'

'I see.'

Moses returned with the attaché case. His mother unlocked it and took out an envelope containing two documents.

'This is my late husband's. He assumed his father was either Huguenot or came from Italy... or somewhere in the Mediterranean, but both his parents died when he was four and he had no relatives. He was adopted but kept his name. I also have those papers if you would like to see them. His adoptive father is dead and mother too frail to question, so I would appreciate it if she was not bothered.'

Mr Alcott examined every document handed to him with a forensic eye.

'I was born in the church hall because there was a storm at the time,' Moses announced brightly. 'Would you like to see the card the minister's wife sent?'

'I am sure that will not be necessary, Moses. After all, if we were this family Mr Alcott is trying to track down, he must be aware that the first thing anyone wishing to disappear would do, is change their name.'

Yes, wondered Moses silently, why didn't his parents change their name? His mother had changed hers to that of his father to follow the convention of the outside world and a different name from that of Olandas went on her forged birth certificate. As the true deviousness adults were capable of occurred to Moses, he said nothing.

Mr Alcott handed the certificates back to his mother. 'You are right of course. That would have been the first thing they would have done when applying for a ration book.' He hesitated. 'But then, you didn't apply for one, did you?'

She smiled a little too sweetly. 'Otherwise you would have no doubt visited us much sooner.'

'Why didn't you apply for a ration book?'

'We are strict vegetarians and our needs very basic. Having been left a generous bequest, we could afford to buy directly from local growers who were glad of the extra income.'

'I'm not sure that was quite legal.'

'It is the nearest I ever came to the black market. And I rather think it is a little late to arrest me now, Mr Alcott - unless that other matter you are unable to discuss has not been resolved to your satisfaction?

'Thank you for the tea, Mrs Oradonte.' As he turned to leave, he had an afterthought. 'Where was it you intend to move to again?'

'Another place by the sea, this time on a cliff.'

Chapter 9

Bill Petersen had been potholing for 20 years, yet had never encountered these subterranean meanders leading to the deep water course cut by a Jurassic river. Now safely above the water table and with no threat of a deluge to flood his escape route, he wriggled through a gap into a large cave.

This had not been hewn out by water action, but power tools. Yet it was so ancient, the walls encrusted with calcites and the ceiling dripping with stalactites, it must have been prehistoric. Even stranger were the solid, ancient doors securing several recesses cut into the rock.

As Bill's torch beam swept about the cave it threw into terrifying relief monsters, peculiar horned angels and feathered dragons. He would have scurried back through the gap in alarm if some benign genie hadn't sensed his presence and bathed the place in a warm, welcoming light.

It revealed statues of alien entities entwined about supporting pillars or bursting from the rock as though frozen on some errand for a troll king. Bill had been through hundreds of grottoes tiled with shells and skulls, or with characters from Greek mythology installed in every crevice: none of them had contained anything like this. These subterranean guardians were even furled about the surrounds of some wooden doors long fossilised into the walls.

The caver recovered sufficiently from his amazement to tug the line and let his companion know he was safely through. He then clambered up onto a ramp, again too cleanly cut to have been worked with prehistoric flint tools or stag antlers. The miners who had excavated this could have taught modern civil engineers a thing or two.

Bill was too elated at making the discovery and the prospect of the promised reward to remain intimidated or question how the mysterious cave came into existence. Yet, he still felt uneasy. Although there were no human remains here, the cave seemed haunted. Something resented trespassers. He tugged the line again to tell Nat to come through - the experienced caver would have welcomed the company of the Wookey Hole Witch for reassurance at that moment.

The beam of Nat's torch shone across the cave.

'What've we got, Bill?' he called out. He was one of life's optimists and always calculated the reward before seeing the chasm it was suspended over.

'Just what they said we'd find.'

Nat pulled himself into the cavern. 'Bloody hell, Bill! Anything down here's bound to be treasure trove.'

'We're just being paid to plant her transmitter, not dig anything up.'

'What will they pay as for keeping our mouths shut?'

'We're getting paid enough already. Don't push it.'

'I'd like to know what's behind them doors.'

As Nat explored he activated an ancient sensor and a sudden spotlight projected monstrous shadows onto the cave walls.

Bill had seen enough. 'This is too fucking weird! Let's plant the thing and get the hell out of here.'

Nat pulled the transmitter from his knapsack and took it to the steps where they had been instructed to install it. 'Find of a lifetime and it has to be something that would frighten the shit out of Indiana Jones.'

'If your bowels are feeling that way, I'm first out.'

After wedging the device firmly in a gap between two steps, Nat switched it on. 'Let's hope the poltergeist down here don't take exception to it.'

But Bill was already wriggling back through the gap to the subterranean world he could cope with.

Chapter 10

Fairdamon had been deserted for over 40 years; not even hardened vandals daring to breach the walls emblazoned with posters warning of anthrax. So many likely yobs had it tattooed on their knuckles they must have had some idea what that was.

Where the huge, ornamental gates had once offered a view down to the towers, pinnacles and cupolas of the mysterious town, there was now a solid, tank proof barrier. Any gaps in the perimeter wall had been repaired and, just to be sure, razor wire deterred even the pigeons from perching.

As Sandra Menzies slowly drove her truck along the narrow road that encircled Fairdamon she began to give up any hope of finding the secret entrance in its forbidding fortification, let alone it being large enough to accommodate excavating equipment. Her crew liked nothing more than a spot of demolition, but this contract stipulated that no trace of the break-in should remain. The sharp-featured woman sitting incongruously in the cab beside her was going to make sure about that. Lawyers - what the world could get away with if it weren't for them. However, on this occasion the price was so right Sandra had no qualms about the nefarious adventure, and if anything went wrong the solicitor beside her would ensure a plea of ignorance. The builder's business account had never been so healthy, so and nothing could be allowed to go wrong: she even had a lookout car tailing them just in case - though in case of what, she wasn't quite sure.

'Whose mansion are we raiding then?' Sandra inadvisability asked to lighten the atmosphere.

Yolanda Fearnley paused from studying the labels on an ancient bunch of keys. 'Any chattels you find will be restored to their rightful owner,' was the stern reply. 'If you can reach the vault in question you will see nothing compromising. My two assistants can secure the artefacts. All you need to do is help me pack the crates.'

'Let's hope we can break in then.'

'Mr Oradonte has every confidence in your expertise.' There was an edge to her tone that suggested she had advised against using this particular civil engineering company after checking up on its employees, but had been overruled.

As they circled the wall for the third time, the solicitor was at last able to pinpoint the ancient entrance to Fairdamon. It was overgrown with weeds.

Sandra got out to check it. This old door may have allowed Alice through into Wonderland, but not the generator, drill and diggers. It was just as well she had a crane on standby outside the nearby village.

One of her team cleared away the brambles and nettles hiding the solid wooden doorway and was just revving up a chainsaw to remove it from its hinges when Yolanda Fearnley placed a key in the door's heavy lock and turned it. She managed to ease it open a few inches with the toe of her elegant, totally impractical, high-heeled shoe. Only then did she allow him to push the chainsaw into the gap and cut away an obstructing branch.

Once the door was open the legal team and builders stepped through. The deserted town of Fairdamon was overgrown and circled by swifts that had been nesting for centuries in its ancient eaves.

The intruders cautiously started down, builders' boots stomping a path through the nettles for the high heels and patent leather shoes of the lawyers.

The narrow roads on the outskirts of the town contained steeply tiered, snug, terraced houses with balconies on each level. Every now and then the breeze caught the blades of an ancient windmill bolted to a rooftop, and what might have once been solar panels flapped like distressed mirrors as the wind lifted them free of the pan tiles. An ancient system for collecting rainwater had fractured. The resulting stream had created a gully through which it flowed down the main street to pool itself in the town centre.

But that was not their destination. Yolanda Fearnley consulted an old map and pointed to an inconspicuous archway. Sandra immediately knew that there was no way her digging equipment would get through that either. The wall by some steps leading down into the ground had been demolished, effectively sealing an entrance from casual observation.

The receiver carried by one of the legal team picked up the signal from the transmitter planted by the cavers Bill and Nat. It would take spades, pickaxes and muscle to remove the rubble from the stairs to reach it. Any machinery operating in a confined space this ancient would undermine the surrounding buildings and subterranean roof. So Sandra radioed the drivers of the conspicuous loader with the diggers, drill, and the crane waiting outside Greenbridge Village to return to the yard.

The builders sweated and swore until dusk before reaching the head of the cellar stairs and shaft of a platform lift. Sandra would have sent a couple of her team to wheel the small generator on her truck down so they could have some light to work by if Ms Fearnley hadn't stopped her.

The builder may have been lax in filing her accounts, but understood the value of having a no-claims policy. 'My team is not excavating over that abyss in total darkness.'

The solicitor picked through her ancient bunch of keys and selected a small, grooved cylinder which she pushed into a ceramic panel that had been cleared of rubble. With one half turn, the throb of a generator vibrated from far below and the place was flooded with light.

'How the hell..?' Sandra's manager started.

'Please don't ask me. I have no idea,' said Ms Fearnley.

Sandra could see that her crew were becoming spooked. She had sent them into tunnels, through crumbling Victorian sewers, and into coffer dams holding back tons of mud, but this strange place was creepier than a vampire's crypt.

The solicitor peered down into the cavern far below it. 'The platform lift appears to be free of rubble so should also be operative.'

'Don't do it boss!' Sandra's manager protested.

But she had no choice; a contract was a contract and she couldn't ask her employees to take the risk, however comprehensive their insurance cover.

'I shall go down with you,' announced the solicitor.

'In those heels?'

'As the debris has not blocked the lift shaft, I see no problem.'

The civil engineer could see several, but had better sense than to argue with a lawyer, and the less her team knew the less culpable they would be if anything went wrong.

Yolanda Fearnley referred to a small diagram, selected another key, pushed it into a slot, and gave it a full turn. They could hear the platform lift below move. 'We have been assured that the ramp at the bottom is quite clear. Shall we go?'

'Oh no you don't! Sandra told her. 'We take the steps down and send your stuff back up on that lift.'

'Very well.' The solicitor knew better than to argue and turned to her assistants. 'Place the crates on the platform when it arrives and send it back down.' She handed one of them the lift key.

'Give them a walkie-talkie, Garry. You may need to show them how to use one,' Sandra turned to Mrs Fearnley and added sweetly, 'but there won't be any extra charge.'

Suppressing any misgivings for the crazy venture, and listening for the snapability of the lawyer's heels as she led the way, Sandra was too preoccupied to wonder about the ancient engineering that made Fairdamon's subterranean world possible.

The light increased as the two women zigzagged

their way down several flights of surprisingly intact stairs surrounding the platform lift shaft. That may have once carried people, but without a cage was best suited to containers.

Despite signing a non-disclosure agreement, Bill Peterson had secretly warned Sandra what to expect when they descended into Fairdamon's subterranean world. He didn't want anyone else to receive the fright he experienced on entering the cave. Notwithstanding, as the two women stepped from the ramp leading into the large cavern, they could only catch their breath and wonder at the exotic statues entwining pillars or bursting from walls as though ready to set about unwelcome intruders.

Sandra and Ms Fearnley waited just long enough to be sure that nothing in the shadows moved. The builder was tempted to take out her Instamatic and record a few snaps of this sinister Aladdin's cave, but a frown from the solicitor warned her against it.

After Sandra double-checked that there was no obstruction around the lift platform and the cable lifting it had not been misaligned, it was sent up to collect the crates filled with bubble wrap and polystyrene chips. By the number that came back down, the hoard they were plundering was going to prove larger than Sutton Hoo's. She then joined Ms Fearnley who was referring to the labels on her keys before going to the furthest vault and turning a complex sequence of tumblers in its lock. Sandra helped pull the heavy door open.

Both women could only gasp in amazement at what was illuminated by the flickering light that came on as they entered. It was a treasure chamber filled with such beautiful artefacts the builder was reluctant to pass over its threshold. 'What is this stuff?'

'My client's inheritance.' The solicitor turned to face Sandra. 'It's all right. My firm are satisfied that he is the legal owner.'

'It's astounding... Very strange and astounding...'

'Quite.'

'I think it better no one in my team sees this stuff,' Sandra reluctantly advised. 'I don't doubt their honesty when it comes to tools and overtime, but this must be worth a fortune. And I know how tempted Tweety Pie and Michaela can be when it comes to anything that glitters. Had to rap their knuckles more than once.'

Ms Fearnley was well aware of the light-fingered natures of the two mentioned. 'It is worth a fortune, though probably not for the reason you think.'

'You're not tempted?'

'Believe me, it would be impossible to sell. Don't touch anything that looks like glass. It's too fragile to handle.'

Sandra helped the solicitor carefully wrap each piece in bubble wrap.

It took most of the night to pack the artefacts and send the crates up for the solicitor's assistants to seal with security tags. While they worked on, the team of builders found surprisingly comfortable, albeit musty, accommodation in the nearby houses to catnap in.

As dawn broke the crates were carried through the ghost town to the other side of the wall.

The future of her company ensured, Sandra was happy to put the escapade to the back of her mind and stop wondering how Ms Fearnley not only survived the night unruffled in a tight-fitting suit and high heels, but how she managed to stay awake long enough to go on and check all the items into a bank vault.

Chapter 11

Katherine Delahaye could not take her gaze off the tall man as he passed by. She had never seen a human quite like him before, with his straight, unsmiling features and silver hair flecked by golden strands that caught the sunlight.

To her mortification he came closer, as though equally fascinated by the florist; close enough for Kath to feel as though she could swim in the liquid grey blue ocean of his gaze.

Aware that they were in a public place and analysing each other a little too intently, they involuntarily looked away. He passed on to a secluded table at the far end of the restaurant patio, and she returned to the salad that had just been served. Passion, or some other unexpected emotion, had hijacked Kath's appetite. She began to eat all the same, slyly snatching glances across the patio. The enigma with the silver hair hardly touched his herbal tea as he waited. Halfway through her salad Kath saw a woman in a smart business suit and ridiculously high heels go to him, pull a maroon folder from her briefcase, hand it over without a word, and then leave.

Kath was a well adjusted young(ish) woman not usually consumed by curiosity with matters that it didn't concern her, yet the gold monogram gleaming on the folder drew her gaze like the sparkle of its owner's hair. To her acute embarrassment, the way he studiously avoided gazing back suggested the interest was mutual.

Moses Oradonte had startled himself by being attracted to a woman whose existence obviously revolved around flowers, the perfume and pollen of which were the bane of his life. Despite the fragrance of freesias, carnations and lilies on her silk blouse he had detected as he passed her, he wanted to draw closer. Katherine Delahaye radiated an empathic charisma that was wasted on other mere mortals. They would have looked at her rounded, not especially beautiful, face lacking any trace of makeup and come to a snap judgement. The florist was slim and trim enough to satisfy modern obsessions with size, yet wore flat heeled shoes and practical, loose fitting slacks which hardly emphasised her figure. It was obvious that this was a woman who did not give a toss for sad people whose lives revolved around nothing deeper than appearance, which made her all the more irresistible to Moses. However much he told his normally calm libido to behave, if he didn't act now this remarkable woman would be gone forever.

Their subtle encounter had not escaped the attention of the eagle-eyed waiter. Matchmaking customers was not part of the service. But - what the hell - Moses Oradonte, despite being sour faced and taciturn, always gave an obscenely large tip and the woman had the warmest of smiles for him each time she came in. All it took was a raised eyebrow and a card with a gold monogram that matched the one on the maroon folder to appear in Moses' immaculately manicured fingers. It was handed to the waiter without a word - this customer seldom spoke. The card was discreetly placed on a tray beneath Kath's bill and taken to her. Endeavouring not to show any reaction, she turned it over. On the back of the card was immaculately scrawled, "The same place in three hours?" and then, without so much as a glance in her direction, the tall enigma with the amazing hair discreetly rose and left, leaving his usual, obscenely large tip.

Kath was fazed for a moment. A glance at the waiter merely elicited a mischievous shrug, so she pushed the card into her purse and wondered if she dare excuse herself for an hour, leaving it up to a geriatric uncle and barely literate teenager to close her flower and china shop. How many customers could they alienate? Probably far fewer than she had done when standing for election as an eco-councillor in a staunchly Conservative ward. As soon as her winning smile on the green posters had appeared, her car dependent, middle-class clientele began buying their bouquets from Tesco, leaving her business to rely on stately home functions, upmarket restaurants, and hanging baskets. That was several years ago, and some still hadn't forgiven her.

At five o'clock exactly Kath returned to find the same table decorated with a mauve candle and centrepiece of palm fronds. What, no romantic flowers? Did her prospective date have hay fever so badly he couldn't look a gerbera in the stamen? One glance at those straight, stern features told her that this man's face would have probably cracked in half if he had sneezed. Was he aware of what he was letting himself in for? Kath had been known to start debates on traffic congestion so heated they were sometimes only ended by the opposition threatening to call out the riot squad.

At last the enigma spoke.

'I understand that you are a local councillor with firm views about the environment?'

'Was voted out last year. Leaves me a lot more time to water the pansies and make nests for bumblebees.'

She would have been perversely disappointed if he hadn't bothered to check up on her. Kath's soul should have sank. From experience, she knew her politics were something that should always be broken gently, especially to the owners of gas-guzzling cars, but something told her that this was not a suitor to be influenced by such minor matters.

'Please sit down. '

'Thank you.' Kath wondered if she should have changed into something more glamorous as the candle flame perversely illuminated the nail varnish that had become cracked by bundling up woody stems. She drew her hands out of the incriminating light and asked, 'Where did the name Oradonte come from?'

'Possibly a misspelling somewhere back in the mists of time.'

It was obviously an evasion, so gratifyingly he was hiding something worthy of curiosity.

'And the Moses wasn't inflicted on you by a vicar who had a rush of Old Testament fervour over the font?'

She shouldn't have said it, but Kath sensed that this man would have only been embarrassed by an apology, unlike many a potential paramour who had been sent running at the prospect of having an acerbic woman with a wit that could grate parmesan in tow for the rest of their lives.

'The name Moses was unusual because we were all heretics.'

The agnostic in Kath was reassured to learn that, though began to wonder what sort of fish she had landed.

She would find out what drawbacks her catch entailed all in good time - there was always bound to be one. At least he knew something about antiques, and flowers if only because of the potency of their perfume and pollen.

And so began that strange, intense relationship punctuated by asthma attacks with a lover who gradually became reluctant to leave the security of his own private domain, even for morning coffee, unless summoned by equally mysterious accountants and solicitors, and only then if they sent a car with clouded windows. There were to be no more candlelit assignations under the watchful gaze of a well intentioned waiter.

Kath had been in business in for some while, yet had never come across the Dickensian deference of the people who managed the affairs that Moses was so secretive about. Even stranger, he often waited until night fell before venturing out of the front door.

The neighbours did not notice Kath coming and going as she had the key to the garden gate and French windows of the study which looked out onto a moss garden lovingly tended by Patsy, the cheery gardener who often wore a daisy in her sun hat.

It wasn't until Kath had been totally ensnared by this emotional bond that she realised most other women would have ran as soon as they saw the mythical beasts guarding the front gate. They were weirdly alien and Kath hadn't a clue where they had originated from. They probably came from the same never never land as her lover.

Chapter 12

Lottie Freeman believed that after the years in the NHS spent dealing with perfectly fit patients who claimed to be at death's door, that should have qualified her for a doctorate in patience as well as medicine. For every gravely ill person grateful to enter her surgery, there were at least two who refused to stop smoking, drinking or go on a diet or demand to see a consultant. Lottie had never misprescribed or refused to treat anyone, though telling quite a few patients they were wasting her and the National Health's time did generate complaints about her lack of bedside manner. Michael Freeman would have been gratified to know that this side of his daughter's character was more Valkyrie than ministering angel.

The last straw was the obese patient who took exception to being told that she was overweight. Having dealt with too many who refused to accept that body size was directly correlated to the amount of calories consumed, Lottie Freeman decided to call it a day. She was a good doctor and knew that there were many willing to pay for her medical know-how. Let the NHS deal with major surgery and life's losers so she could be generously remunerated for putting up with wealthy hypochondriacs and their foibles.

Her mother disapproved of her daughter's mercenary outlook and regarded her private practice as more of a retirement hobby, like that of her older brother, Fred, who spent his time building model ships. He had spent a contented and uneventful life as a country accountant and intended to spend a contented and uneventful retirement. With luck, Lottie would never discover the truth about her father, the only thing to ever give him sleepless nights. Fred had managed to keep the terrible revelation from their mother for so long, and hoped the papers relating to it would be fortuitously mislaid in the files of Chapman, Chapman and Son, the family solicitors.

Lottie, despite her brother's best endeavours, could tell that there was some dark family secret that needed to be kept from their frail, aged mother at all costs, as easily as when a patient was withholding something. So, when Penelope Freeman died, well into her nineties, one way or another, Lottie expected to learn the truth.

After leaving the funeral reception she sat with Fred and his wife, Maddie, going through the boxes of mementos, photos, and documents; 90 years of memorabilia, much of it lovingly wrapped by their late lamented, and enigmatic, family butler. Amongst the lockets, letters, corsages, brooches and theatre programmes there were none of those formal visiting cards with embossed crowns Lottie could recall so vividly, mainly because they were inscribed in German and she was furious at not being able to read them. All the photos of those forbidding and fur clad guests the house had entertained when she was an infant were also missing. Lottie's medical antenna for missing forms was alerted and Maddie held her breath in trepidation as she could see the cogs of suspicion turning behind her sister-in-law's expression. When thwarted, Lottie could be so waspish it was almost possible to hear the annoyed buzzing which made her one of the unlikeliest people to be in the medical profession. Horse doctors had a better bedside manner. The mystery was why people queued to get on her list of private patients, and not all of them were masochists. The only explanation must have been that her talent for diagnosis far exceeded the expertise of most GPs - and numerous consultants - and had saved many from premature decrepitude or death.

Lottie Freeman's exasperation was, on the whole, reserved for those who invited it. With age, the energy to intimidate remained, even if the inclination had waned. The more she learnt, the more remarkable life seemed, until it occurred to her that most unlikely conspiracy theories, from aliens under the ice caps to the suppression of the pill that turned water into petrol, had an element of truth. Fred knew that his sister's single-mindedness came from their father; though her sense of justice was more primeval. He had frequently glanced at the family photos and wondered at how such a Valhalla warrior could have been his little sister. Even her tightly curled hair still frizzed out with an attitude of its own and defied any attempt to straighten it. Most disconcerting, was the way his wife, Maddie, secretly admired the strong, uncompromising personality of her sister-in-law. Lottie was certainly not the friend she could take to a W. I. meeting or bridge. Yet, when Dr Freeman had been a National Health GP, Maddie had occasionally enjoyed accompanying her on rounds to see how problem families retreated from the hard glance and the deft way she loaded a hypo. While Maddie's nursing experience enabled her to reassure nervous patients and change the odd dressing, Lottie went about her medical business as though the body on the bed was an inconvenient distraction.

There was a prolonged pause before Lottie shattered the silence that had fallen over Fred and Maddie's living room. 'So, where's our father's death certificate then?'

Fred looked at his sister blandly as though she had just asked how the cat was recovering from an ear infection. 'No idea. Probably in here somewhere.'

'No it isn't. Mother wouldn't shove something like that at the bottom of a box.'

'Why is it so important?'

'It's important because it's not here.' Lottie assumed her interrogator's glare. 'Why isn't it here, Fred?'

Her brother fidgeted uneasily at being caught out after a lifetime of keeping the secret, and said nothing.

44

Maddie wanted to know as well. 'Yes Fred, what did your father really die of?'

'He went down with The Voyager when it sank.'

'Bollocks!' snapped Lottie. 'No such ship!'

Fred's jaw dropped.

'I checked it out,' she accused. 'Now mother's dead it's about time us women were told father's dirty secret.'

'Oh Lottie... you really don't...'

'Don't patronise us, you goggle-eyed, number pusher. After 70 years nothing can be that secret.' Then Lottie had second thoughts. 'Or can it..?'

Fred flushed with discomfort. 'The truth had to be buried for security reasons. If the Secret Service hadn't done that, our family would have been dispossessed and plunged into penury. We would probably have ended up digging turnips.'

'Speak for yourself. I'd have sold aspirin on the black market.'

'I know you would, you were a mercenary madam even then.'

'Oh Fred,' Maddie joined in, 'we have to know now. I'll pour turps in your model glue if you don't tell us.'

Fred, now cornered and near to tears, admitted, 'I can't. Only our solicitor has the authority.'

'Why pay Chapman to do it?'

'You're wealthy enough. Make an appointment.'

'Can I come?' asked Maddie.

'No,' Fred said firmly. 'It will be on condition it stays with blood relatives.'

'I'll tell you all about it afterwards,' Lottie whispered.

Chapter 13

As Kath had anticipated, life with Moses Oradonte turned out to be strange. She became aware that he didn't see the world in the same way as other people and had the ability to look below the surfaces they barely glanced at. Personalities were an open book to Moses, however well others thought their true intentions were concealed. He had the same understanding of animals, which no doubt explained his vegetarianism. How could a person consume the flesh of a creature they were able to comprehend on a level Dr Doolittle would have envied?

And yet the man, for all his well-spoken elegance and incongruously fair, saturnine looks, was unfathomable in a quixotic way. Having tilted at emotional windmills he knew, deep down, that nothing about the absurd reality he found himself in would ever be resolved. In a different incarnation Moses would have been a mystic, a martyr, or Flying Dutchman adrift in a dimension that refused to accept his otherworldliness.

Sometimes, when Kath looked at her lover unawares, she could picture an ocean; not calm waves glinting in the setting sun, but a Mandelbrot abstract in never-ending motion, more foam than water. It was an inexplicable impression of someone who had probably never paddled on the nearby beach. If there was anything about him deeply buried in her subconscious, it was best not to draw it out. Moses was complicated enough; adding yet another layer would make him seem even more improbable. But she would never shake the idea that the man belonged to another plane of existence beyond her ken. It was exasperating to love an enigma whose passion was more inferred than apparent.

It wasn't until they had been in the relationship for several years he admitted that his mother actually had a different surname, a convention of whatever unlikely tribe they belonged to, which she had changed it to avoid confusing the locals of the time. Kath sensed there was a little more to it than that. As everything about Moses was already disconcerting enough she never asked about the rest of his family. When in an intense relationship, it's sometimes best not to know too much.

Kath had no doubt that Moses loved her, although his unsmiling expression seldom gave anything away. The small gifts of jewellery and other gewgaws said that this was a man who understood her tastes. She would have felt more comfortable about his expensive presents if he had allowed her to reciprocate in kind, but her business wasn't doing well and she suspected that Moses was ridiculously wealthy despite never flaunting it.

Kath had liked his unusual mother with an aristocratic bearing, and was by her side when she died. Allana Olandas was adroit, interesting and elegant, but old before her time. Yet her hair had remained its natural gold as her son's turned to silver. For as long as Kath had known Moses, his mother had suffered from a chest infection. Despite this, neither of them ever visited a doctor. There was no point in nagging these enigmatic, detached people to trust a mortal medical practitioner. Death seemed of little consequence to them in their own private world where state of mind was more important than the state of health. And when Allana Olandas died, probably from the pain killing potion administered by Moses, it seemed as though she had been released to a greater truth beyond religion or philosophy. Mother and son understood that the nature of existence eluded most people. Kath didn't resent their apparent enlightenment and was content to bask in the light of their mysterious universe without being intimidated. That was probably why she stayed with Moses for so long.

Then Kath fell victim to her hormonal clock. If she

was to have a family, the opportunity was closing fast. It had always been understood that Moses could not give her children due to a genetic problem neither he, nor his mother, would explain.

When she eventually told Moses they had to part, his expression remained immobile, as it always did when he had no intention of giving away his feelings. He only insisted on one condition; that she would raise her family, and never see him again.

So, when she left his closest companion became his ever present, industrious gardener.

Chapter 14

Patsy Dowland was a jolly soul. In her world of flowers, herbs, weeds, and vegetables she floated above the humdrum concerns of others. A derogatory remark about immigrants would trigger an explanation about the labour required to pick fruit and cut cabbages. Pointing out that inexpensive Western food was dependent on cheap imported labour had become an effective way of ensuring that person did not attempt to make blinkered conversation again.

With only one exception, Patsy had no time for wilting humanity; she had more empathy with plants, Nature's bounty for the ungratefully deluded who believed vegetables sprang up ready packed in polystyrene trays.

Moses Oradonte must have shared his gardener's point of view despite Nature's perfume swamping his olfactory senses, because he allowed her to transform the grounds beyond the sanctuary of his moss garden into insect heaven. Like Kath, Patsy did not totally understand his allergies, just accepted them as another of her employer's oddities. They seemed all the more baffling when she occasionally caught him watching, entranced, as a butterfly took a wrong turning and alighted on the green velvet of his private retreat and flutter there, jewel like, before realising that there was no nectar to be had from moss.

Patsy and her husband had settled down in a mobile home at the bottom of Moses Oradonte's huge garden, which he had invited them to use after their terraced house had been flooded several years before. The couple could see no point in moving back to a place which was liable to be flooded yet again and faced a road increasingly choked with traffic. The garden overlooked the sea, was in walking distance of their allotment and quiet apart from birdsong and the occasional 'pop' of guns on the army firing ranges. Best of all, it was rent free because Moses insisted it come with the job. It was a good way of ensuring he kept the best gardener he ever had. Like the prefabs of the last war, which were meant to be temporary, the mobile home's low ceiling and snug accommodation would become too comfortable to leave for cold bricks and mortar.

When left to her own devices, Patsy planted, pruned and weeded from morning till night. Away from Nature's realm she became a lost soul, like a disorientated mud skipper trying to find its way back to a pool in the mangrove swamp and, like Moses Oradonte, she found other human beings an acquired taste.

His moss garden had taken years to nurture, but when it was mature he could open his study's French windows and be engulfed by its green, sound absorbing duvet. The regular attention the moss required gave Patsy a view into a personal world where other mortals were seldom allowed. Only Kath had ever got that close, and she would chat about everything, except Moses.

After Kath left Patsy could always recall the last discussion they had about a new begonia hybrid, and the greenhouse where Kath intended to grow her own house plants. It was a pity she never saw the moss garden at its peak. After years of continual spraying and replacing bald patches, the refuge of natural velvet was subtly illuminated so Moses could sit outside in the evenings. Patsy had no idea whether this made any difference to his deteriorating chest condition or deadened the din of the outside world that so disturbed him. That was dealt with by Wendy, his secretary cum-housekeeper. She was discrete, likeable, exotic, and efficient at fending off the world's intrusions. To all appearances Moses seemed content, but Patsy was aware of the small locked drawer in his desk from which he occasionally took a phial and needle.

Chapter 15

Kath could never admit to herself whether she had left Moses to find a man who could give her a family or because she had set eyes on Neville who, at first glance, was hardly a procreating machine. Her attraction to this fair-haired, slightly balding man with an amiable expression a less charitable person might have taken to be dim-witted made no more sense than why she was drawn to Moses. The men were total opposites. Moses only spoke when necessary and never chatted; Neville probably lived for chance encounters and comfortable conversation. The nearest Moses came to handicrafts was stapling the pages of his mysterious and interminable translation together. Neville, it transpired, was accomplished at plumbing, carpentry, electrical wiring, decorating, and welding; skills learnt as a shipwright's fitter; not that Kath would have trusted him to row her across the Mersey in a dinghy. She would have assumed him to be just another benign male blundering about a complicated world when they first collided with each other at that garden centre. He had been unable to see over the hydrangea just purchased for a sister with a spare tub of ericaceous compost, and she was too busy scrutinising the cafe's menu for vegetarian options to notice him coming.

Moses' aversion to any perfume had frequently driven Kath to find refuge in such local floral outlets as her own florist shop was too far away. Perhaps the other thing that attracted her to Neville was that, despite having a poor sense of smell, he had an affinity with plants as well as plush cabin fittings.

After they had returned the hydrangea to its pot, Neville immediately took the blame and insisted on buying Kath coffee. She could tell by his guileless manner that he was still single, despite being almost her age, and was surprised that no woman had snapped up this amiable, multitalented handyman. Then again, he did tick all the boxes that marked a man as "uncool". He had no mobile phone, wore a sleeveless Fair Isle pullover, drove a two stroke Reliant, had a mother with five cats, and lived in a flat over a Chinese take-away. Neville was such an extraordinarily contented soul, apparently unfazed by anything, Kath felt that it was like opening a cardboard box, slightly battered in transit, to find it filled with Dutch carnations. More fool other women for not bothering to lift the lid.

Neville was hardly an impulsive man, and was taken aback to find he was attracted to the slightly older woman with the mischievous sparkle in her eyes. Other women he had attempted to show interest in frequently turned out to be mercenary or just plain silly behind all the self-conscious artifice and never ending texting on their mobiles. Experience told him that, to assess the intellect of someone you had just met, just listen to the conversations they held with their mobile phones as though the rest of the world couldn't hear.

After much soul-searching, house hunting, and meeting relatives, Kath and Neville decided to take the plunge. A contract of partnership was drawn up, witnessed, and rings exchanged, much to the disappointment of Neville's mother who wanted a wedding opportunity to wear her best brocade suit while she could still get into it. So the couple talked her vicar round into blessing the union instead of marrying them. As the cleric had already married several gay couples, it seemed inevitable that convention would turn itself inside out.

So Neville's sisters and mother, Kath's uncle and her florist shop staff, had the opportunity to party in their best frocks. Kath's only regret was that Moses couldn't be persuaded to attend. Although the man had no resentment in his soul, the scent of Lilium regale and hair lacquer would have paralysed him.

So, in a house fitted out in shipshape fashion and filled with flowers, Kath and Neville began a family while her hormones still obliged.

Chapter 16

Dr Duncan Parfait was one of those slightly overweight, full-featured men in their mature 40s who had looks that, in a woman, would have been called voluptuous. He was totally unaware of the disorganised, verging on shambolic, charisma that women found so attractive and preferred to believe that they clustered about him for his huge knowledge of the ancient world and the vigour with which he disseminated his subject. Carol, his economist partner, allowed him to believe it; the last thing she wanted was the archaeologist to become aware of his allure and run off with the next woman able to quote Herodotus.

Carol and Duncan's mews apartment was large enough to compartmentalise for the requirements of their very different professions. Despite this, he had never comprehended the meaning of demarcation and his research papers, specimens, and manuscripts managed to crop up anywhere from the bathroom to fridge, and all points in between. Carol had once arrived in Cologne to give a lecture on the Napoleonic banking system only to find the synopsis for a volume on Nubian relics in the binder. She had to assume Duncan had gone to his publisher with a proposal about early 19th century European economics. Without Rolf Baker, his researcher, to prompt him, she could only wonder at how that encounter must have panned out.

As well as being a firm anchor to counter the turbulent debates he provoked on and off the TV screen, Duncan also found Carol indispensable for dealing with his fan mail. The archaeologist, who had unearthed some of the most pornographic images the ancient world could offer, was unaccountably embarrassed by salacious messages expressing appreciation of various parts of his anatomy and never asked what replies she sent. Needless to say, the infatuated culprits did not contact him again.

Carol's commitments as a lecturer on economics meant that she was away much of the time, confident that everything would be the same whenever she returned from Dubai or LA. Not that she couldn't have taken up with a Saudi prince or Greek playboy - she really was voluptuous - but this economist preferred the undemanding company of someone who covered their apartment's walls with post-it reminders and frequently managed make Word crash before saving a file. Just as Duncan seemed like an open book to her, without warning the odd page would fall drop out to reveal the barely legible, exotic side to her partner. Sinbad would have been impressed. Somewhere in Duncan's immediate ancestry some Polynesian antecedent had passed on the gene for oceanic adventure and lust for mythical worlds. A European gene countered that it was all bunkum, of course, and demanded he pour authoritative scorn on those who believed in Lemuria and the lost continent of Atlantis. His latest book was more scornful than its predecessors, and even raised the hackles of his stalwart, and otherwise stoical, researcher. Rolf Baker claimed that Duncan's efforts to disprove ancient myths were due to an increasingly desperate attempt to deny the gene that believed in fairies. Despite that, the younger man got on well with his employer and could ill afford to lose the income.

'What have you done with my orange folder, my precious?'

Carol heard Duncan's awful impression of Sméagol from the bedroom; it didn't help her attempts to secure the butterfly to her diamond earring. 'Put it in the bin with all your other junk, sweetie!'

'It's okay - found it!'

'Now go launch the book, honeybun! You know the way to Waterstones, don't you?'

'Of course I do!'

Of course he didn't. He was going to take a taxi as he usually did. After Rolf had found the Rat and Compass, he usually needed a taxi back as well, though Rolf always managed to blunder his way home after a surfeit of light ale and discussion on contentious historical theories. Put the weedy young man in the middle of a wilderness with a trowel and compass and he would not only discover archaeological gold, but always navigate his way home as though he had his own inbuilt satnav.

Carol had left for the Eurostar by the time Duncan was presentable enough for his public. They usually expected to wait for the disorganised media presenter anyway, so teasing their anticipation had become something of a ritual.

When he arrived at Waterstones there was a gratifyingly long queue, not yet long enough for irritation to set in.

Duncan spent the next three hours signing his new title, 'Excavating Lost Knowledge', and fending off conspiracy theories about the ancient world, with pure charisma because doctrine seldom worked. He had done this so often he was virtually on auto drive, smiling benignly and trotting out well worn platitudes in his plummy TV tones. Then, from nowhere, a tall, enigmatic man appeared, holding out his book to be signed. The straight, distinguished features were immobile so Duncan was unable to categorise him as a devotee or critic. In fact, he wasn't so sure this customer fitted into any category he had ever encountered before.

Duncan signed the title page with more care than usual, leaving no comment. For some reason this customer filled him with an apprehension he had not experienced since jumping off the high board for the first time. Briefly glancing away to acknowledge the overweening admiration of a fan, the man was gone when he turned back.

By the time Rolf arrived to see how well the book was doing, Duncan was ready for a lunch and stiff drink in the Rat and Compass.

Chapter 17

The evening air was filled with the scent of orange blossom, rosemary, and eau de cologne mint throwing off clouds of appreciation for the drenching Patsy had given them before leaving to weed her allotment.

Moses sneezed as their perfume leached into the sanctuary of his moss garden. That high wall blanketed in green velvet would never be high enough to block out the intrusion of a world filled with traffic fumes and Nature busily infusing any remaining gaps. It wasn't a mere pathogen that had killed his family, it was busy, busy humanity, saturating the atmosphere with the pollutants they seemed to thrive on.

Poor Kath, despite being so tolerant and forbearing, never really understood: Moses didn't truly comprehend the curse of his genetic legacy either. He had never known his parent's walled town where the pace of life was considered, needless noise forbidden, and intelligent conversation compulsory. He was descended from a culture that had been able to thrive in the isolation of its own world of thought and dreams because of fortunes judiciously invested over the centuries. Now there was nothing to show for their splendid existence but a bank vault full of pointless treasure the world was not ready to see. Moses, sole survivor of the community that had created it all, was the only guardian of the truth. He hoped he would not live long enough to witness the egocentric view modern humans had of the ancient world being overturned. He preferred not to know how they would react.

The wisdom of Fairdamon was, "Let go of this reality and return to the dimension where thoughts no longer exist. Only intentions and creativity matter, and time is a delusion." But Moses did not live in the sanctuary of Fairdamon. He lived in a world of noise, misconceptions, and self-centred futility. Despite the claim of his ancestors that reality was an illusion, something deep in the core of his being insisted that their wonderful achievements could not be allowed to fade into oblivion. How would his trim little solicitor deal with the treasure filled bank vault when he was dead if he did not bequeath it to someone? Could the young Ms Kandy shoulder the responsibility of cataloguing and finding homes for all the impossible relics? Her mind, however lucid, would never be focussed enough to deal with the inevitable fallout when specialists discovered the true nature of the pieces. Yolanda Fearnley, her predecessor, would have shaken the antiquities world by the heels and demanded it pay attention, but she had long gone. One gin too many and tumble down unforgiving steps at Inns of Court had sent her to the great judge in the sky where her steely heart was no doubt weighed against the feather of justice. In his own way, Moses hoped the devourer of souls went hungry that night.

There was only one person knowledgeable and subjective enough to take on that task. Disorganised in all other regards, his obsessively thought out arguments against such implausible places as Fairdamon meant that he was subconsciously desperate to be persuaded that magical, ancient realms actually existed.

Yes, Dr Duncan Parfait would be the world's last chance to discover the truth about Fairdamon.

Chapter 18

One moment there was glorious sunshine, the next mist had rolled in across the sea like an unfurling duvet.

When Meg started to pack away the picnic plates it was too much for six-year-old Angie.

'We can't go now!' she screeched.

'Don't you shout at your gran like that, you little cow!' Liz screeched back at her daughter.

Tyrone, strapped in his pushchair after tormenting a herring gull with a prawn and nearly losing a finger, decided to join in with a prolonged wail penetrating enough to summon Neptune, while baby Donnie sat watching the family circus with bemused contentment.

'Oh, for pity's sake!' Liz was now shouting louder than her children. 'What is wrong with you two? We've been here all afternoon! It's time to go!'

Meg's ageing ears could never deal with these tantrums and she decided to escape. 'I'll get the car. You can pack the things away.' And without waiting for the inevitable protest, dashed off. As far as she was concerned, the brats should have been given a planet all of their own where absent fathers were compelled to spend 24 hours of every day dealing with their monstrous offspring. Liz no doubt loved Angie and Tyrone in her own way, yet probably wished she had insisted on condoms.

Though no more than 65, Meg had that haggard look common to heavy smokers. Cigarettes had become an addiction, closely followed by alcohol, after her brief foray into romance. Bearing a daughter when she was 15, only to have her die giving birth to Liz, persuaded her that sex was a quicker way to an early grave than booze and cigarettes. The only way Meg had managed to deal with her loss was by trying to rear Lucy's child as her own daughter. The secret had been kept for so long that Liz's ineptitude at arithmetic meant she never questioned the discrepancy in their ages. Meg had always been her mother. Like the ancient bed linen basket bequeathed by older generations, she accepted her as part of the family furniture. Meg could only wonder at how, having produced the beautiful, bright Lucy, she had managed to rear a granddaughter who turned out to be such a drain on her emotional resources and Social Services. Having to work to support the child had been no excuse. The addiction genie had ensured that she lost the ability to arrange her life in a sensible way. Meg would sometimes glance at Liz and wonder what her long gone father must have been like. The girl was nothing like her mother, the pretty, delicate Lucy doomed to an early grave, but unable to wear sensible shoes or anything but skimpy tops, even in midwinter. Meg believed that Liz was subconsciously trying to attract men like her unknown father - she had certainly managed to keep illegitimacy in the family.

By the time that Meg had reached the car and lit a cigarette, Angie was stomping off in rage, making Liz totter after her in ridiculously high heels. From a safe distance it looked more like a pantomime than a minor family drama but then, when Meg thought about it, the machinations of her family should have been put on the stage as a warning against all the indiscretions she had ever committed. However reluctant to admit it, she knew with the benefit of hindsight that this was payback for her own bad management.

Angie's tantrum had turned into enraged flight mode, probably just to make her inadequate mother chase after her. Meg continued to watch with detached interest - why waste a good cigarette to intervene in something she would only end up taking the blame for?

By the time Angie had disappeared into the descending mist, it was too late. The child had played the little girl lost before to get attention and, as far as other adults who didn't know her were concerned, it usually worked. This time was different; the tide was coming in fast and, however much the six-year-old understood about manipulating others, she didn't comprehend that the gravitational attraction of the moon could submerge a shore where she had been playing only an hour before.

Meg realised what had happened and cursed. 'Oh shit..!' She stubbed out her cigarette and reluctantly went back to join her.

Liz was dashing backwards and forwards, panic stricken. 'Angie! Come back here now you little cow! Don't you try and climb that cliff!'

'Forget it, you know she won't come back. You should have seen the signs,' Meg scolded.

'What am I gonna do mum?'

'What we always end up doing. Use my mobile. I've got the local cop shop on speed dial.'

'They'll tell Social Services this time.'

'Let them. They might give her father some aggravation as well.'

'She could fall down a hole, or get cut off by the tide - and what if she tries to climb the cliff?'

Liz was right. There were plenty of hazards in the crumbling cliff and other nooks and crannies once used as Napoleonic defences. Even a child with such a keen sense of self-preservation wasn't likely to see the danger. Despite all that, Meg wasn't going to be the one to call out the coastguard; the prospect of having to pay for the time wasted by the search party loomed large in her mind. As she barely held body, soul, and battered car together on a state pension and the pittance she received for putting up the awful brood, that wasn't something she was prepared to entertain. Meg had already broken her tenancy agreement for letting the feckless Liz and her kids live in the council flat - that was torment enough.

Chapter 19

The smell of cooking shellfish across the access road mingled with the smoke of burnt English breakfasts impregnating the wooden walls of the Harbour Café. The eating place was little more than a shed bolted to the concrete extension of the sea defences overlooking the slipway where trawlers landed their catches.

The rickety seats outside were bolted down against sudden Channel gusts and unruly customers intent on rearranging the furniture. Herring gulls strutted the adjoining patio roof, aiming ear piercing shrieks at a trawler departing to toss gutted fish entrails into the sea. The café was a handy refuge for fishermen, hardy holidaymakers, and the partially deaf. The odd visit by a well-dressed customer braving tea from a perpetually topped up aluminium pot seldom raised interest. Endeavours were always being made to improve the harbour and antagonising those who might well decide to fund it served no useful purpose, and everyone from artists to tourists who had taken a wrong turning stopped to examine the menu on the blackboard at some time or other.

Wendy had lived in the miasma of dingier places where frequenting cafés risked far worse than curious glances at her immaculate clothes and Filipino features. The smartly dressed man who had joined her was a regular customer and plied his dubious trade with impunity in a world where being hard up was the norm and most ways to make a living acceptable. Not that any of the other customers could afford his services. The illicit substances he dealt in were more closely related to the pharmacy than drugs of the dark alley. The Potion Professor was the dealer for the terminally desperate and hardened hypochondriac. However despicable some viewed his trade, others found in it blessed relief, mental and physical, where the doctor with legal constraints dare not go. The Professor gave value for money, lavishing concern, advice and comfort regardless of transaction. His medical knowledge was phenomenal and access to medicines certainly not legal. The only customer who refused to explain why she needed regular consignments of morphine sat gazing at him across the Formica topped table like an enigmatic Eastern fairy, wafting steam from her instant coffee with a bulging, plain brown envelope. If the Potion Professor hadn't a reputation to think about, his libido would have been aroused.

'Wendy, my delicious dish of dim sum, how is the world treating you?' He removed his trilby as though it might be attracting attention to their murky transaction.

Fortunately this was the sort of café where Health and Safety were more likely to raise objections about the customer's dog which had come from under its table at the scent of something interesting in the Professor's case, than at what it contained. If smuggling had still been rife, the authorities here would have prosecuted vendors for putting chairs and tables on the cobbled pavements outside rather than selling under the counter cigarettes.

'The world has always treated me the same, Professor. It is the people inhabiting it who are not consistent.'

Without the need for their illegal transactions, the drug dealer and sophisticated Filipino would have found that they had much in common beyond the practicalities of survival.

But life's necessities came first.

'The consignment as ordered.' The Potion Professor put a small brown box on the table. 'A slight

adjustment in the price I'm afraid - had to use a
different source. The usual supplier is having her
inventory checked. Be back to normal as soon as the
snoopers have put their calculators away.'

'Price is no object.'

The Professor knew this. Wendy was one of the few
customers to never quibble about money, which made
him all the more curious about the intended recipient.
All he could do was hope that they were addicted as
opposed to terminally ill.

Discreetly pocketing the envelope of money, he
watched as the slight, elegant woman took one sip of
her coffee, and then left to catch a taxi which had
mysteriously arrived without apparently being
summoned.

Chapter 20

Patsy stood in the moss garden, holding the nozzle of a
hose as though trying to decide whether to spray the
moss or if she was clutching the head of a dangerous
snake. Moses could tell that she was bracing herself to
ask something. There was no point in leaving the
woman to suffer pained indecision, so he opened the
French windows of his study.

Patsy turned and glanced guiltily at him. 'You've
never met my friend Meg, have you?'

'Another gardener?'

'Not her. Kills everything. If she stood in a field of
dandelions they would run for cover.'

'She sounds like an odd acquaintance for you to
have?'

'School friend. Her child managed to produce such a
monster it persuaded me it was better to grow things
instead of raising a family.' Patsy stopped.

'And there is a problem with her monster
grandchild?'

'Great grandchild actually, but doesn't know it.' she

noted his raised eyebrow indicating that he didn't really want the explanation. 'She's only six.' It was obvious that Moses wasn't going to ask, so she went on. 'Gone missing on the beach in a heavy mist when it was high tide.'

'When?'

'Yesterday evening.'

'Drowned?' There was nothing in his tone that suggested it might have been just as well, but Moses could tell Patsy was thinking it.

'Little madam's done it before. Probably hiding somewhere to get attention. She's too self interested to go and drown for real.'

'And you would like me to "sniff" her out?'

Patsy wasn't going to allude to his remarkable olfactory senses right away, and was grateful he did it first. Meg's life was going to be hell until the little brat was found. And if Angie had been drowned, the rest of her friend's existence would be spent in an alcoholic haze of self-pity and remorse for not taking the pill when it really mattered.

'All right,' Moses agreed.

'Alright?' Patsy had never believed the man to be heartless, though it still came as a surprise that he agreed so quickly. 'Any ground rules?'

'No screeching or cheap hairspray.'

'Can't guarantee that. I'll just tell Meg to keep Liz and her other brat out of the way.'

'Give me half an hour, and then bring your car round - is it still roadworthy?'

'Oh yes.' Patsy assumed he was referring to the bags of compost that had almost damaged its axle. Fortunately, and somewhat strangely, that was one of the few odours her employer didn't object to.

Moses returned to his study and finished wrapping the exquisitely carved wooden statuette on his desk. Before sealing the box, he inserted a card inscribed with his immaculate handwriting.

When Wendy came in to collect it she was tempted

to give the package a vigorous shake for some reason, uncharacteristic of a person who knew from experience how dangerous curiosity could be. His assistant had that immaculate appearance Moses so admired in a woman and which made him wonder all the more why he had fallen for the casual charms of Kath. As well as a Filipino sense of dress with timeless style, Wendy's English, a little too precise, could wrong foot unwelcome callers and never be denied a refund when requested. She was the ideal guardian of Moses Oradonte's secretive world, never giving away so much as the window cleaner's phone number.

Moses handed her a slip of paper.

'Please use this carrier and insure it for that sum.' Wendy raised an eyebrow. 'It is priceless.'

No longer so inclined to shake the package, Wendy took the dispatch note. 'Very well, Mr Oradonte. I shall do this right away.'

After Wendy left, the full weight of what he was doing descended to briefly crush his confidence. Perhaps the Fairdamons had been right; some mysteries were best kept from egocentric humanity. Truth, however splendid or remarkable, ran the risk of angering minds closeted in their own small boxes. What if undermining their concept of reality had consequences he couldn't anticipate? Thank goodness for the distraction of the lost monster child to divert him from thinking about it.

Chapter 21

The younger Mr Chapman of Chapman, Chapman, and Son had never quite mastered the genteel country style of dealing with eccentric squires and rebellious farmers. His favoured stamping ground was Lincoln's Inn Fields, not sitting behind the ancient mahogany desk on which warrants for arrests had been issued to suppress minor local rebellions. It was even claimed

Judge Jeffreys had signed a few death warrants on its faded maroon top; a tradition that the younger Mr Chapman would have dismissed contemptuously had he not been bound by blood to the ancient line of legal advocates. As the only surviving heir with the name of Chapman (apart from his sister who had become a barrister and made far more money) qualified to carry on the hierarchical business, there he was stuck until he produced another male heir who could eventually inherit the familial millstone. Having successfully concealed that he was gay from the rest of the family, he dolefully accepted that he would be stuck behind that desk well into his 90s. The gimlet-eyed woman facing him could tell his sexual orientation without a compensatory strong handshake or noticing the pink lining of his steel spectacle case.

Her family solicitor's private life was the last thing on Dr Lottie Freeman's mind. She was more focused on finding out what was so secret about her mysterious father that it had to be kept it from his widow at all costs.

Her mother, Penelope Freeman, had come from county stock and inherited the family seat on the death of her parents. Neither of them had approved of Michael Freeman: Conservative they may have been, but not so far right as to sympathise with the Nazis, whatever the sentiments of their aristocratic neighbours. Doing so would have not only been unacceptable, but downright unpatriotic. To them the rise of the Third Reich could only spell disaster for the British Empire.

Penelope had been an uncomplicated young woman, not versed in the way of politics, and more inclined to rescue sparrows and pat dray horses. She would have been horrified had she understood the sinister undercurrents of the society she had been born into. Her parent's opposition to the dark-haired, glamorous young man inveigling his way into her affections was incomprehensible. They were well aware that his artful eye was more on her inheritance than romance. Unfortunately Michael Freeman had powerful friends; undermining the relationship could have proved more disastrous, socially and economically than allowing it. At least they lived long enough to see two grandchildren, the youngest with a glint in the eye that suggested she might eventually turn the tables on the Nazi infiltrator, father or not. Any baby who could scratch the cat back was not going to submit to restricting dogma. It proved some sort of comfort to Penelope's mother before she succumbed to pneumonia, and her father who passed on shortly afterwards from a recurrence of malaria contracted on service during the Great War.

Mr Chapman invited Lottie Freeman to take the seat facing him.

He announced amiably, 'Of course, the information should now be in the public domain anyway, though I suspect those files have long since gone missing.'

'Why?'

'MI5 never did like large explosions they couldn't explain,' he said offhandedly in the vain hope she would not pick up on it.

'Large explosions?'

'I'm afraid I'm unable to say any more. Solicitors still have to abide by some rules, even if those on Twitter ignore them. Matters of such import are best left to Wikileaks.'

'And I'm going to find out what happened to my father on Facebook?'

Lottie's tone was becoming hard and the amiable younger Mr Chapman drew back into the security of his leather chair. 'It is unlikely those who do their research in social networking sites would be interested in the intrigues of the real world unless they are related to three-headed aliens or the colour of some pop star's underwear.'

'What can you tell me about my father then?'

Mr Chapman took a deep breath before announcing,

'He was a Nazi spy.'

Lottie was genuinely taken aback. She had always suspected he had been up to something nefarious, but not anticipated that. 'Good God. Just as well our mother never found out. She was convinced he was a stockbroker with aristocratic German friends.'

'Oh, he was. They just happened to be Nazis and the shares he dealt in had more to do with munitions than commodities.'

'Then why didn't the government confiscate everything the family owned?'

'They had no idea what caused the explosion.'

Lottie became frustrated at the elliptical way information was being offered. 'What bloody explosion?'

'Your father apparently took some blackshirts to investigate a cult called the Companions of Urial. He believed that they possessed a doomsday weapon.'

'Did they?'

'No idea.'

Lottie leaned forward on the mahogany desk. 'So, on the eve of the Second World War my father was a German spy hunting a sect called the Friends of Urial who had a doomsday weapon which may, or may not, have caused an explosion MI5 still can't explain?'

'About sums it up.' The solicitor switched to advice mode. 'Please, Dr Freeman, just be grateful the government of the day took no action that could have left your family ostracised and in poverty.'

'I suppose I'm paying for this advice as well?'

'Please listen to your brother.'

'You can add that pearl of wisdom to his bill.'

'It was all a long while ago.'

'I don't like mysteries.'

The solicitor's soul sank, though he should have realised the futility of wasting his advice on this client. 'Oh dear, your brother did warn me.'

'Fred wouldn't change anything until the tanks were churning up his lawn, and then he'd be more worried about the rockery than invasion. If it doesn't impinge on his cosy little world, it's of no interest.'

Mr Chapman's voice lowered considerably as he confided in a non-professional capacity. 'Be careful, Lottie. It is unlikely something like this would be totally forgotten. All it would take is the wrong question in the wrong place to reactivate MI5's interest.'

'Traitorous bastard or not, I still need to know what happened to my father.'

Reluctantly Mr Chapman jotted an address on a scrap of paper. 'It's a private collection. Mention my name to the librarian - but not too loudly.'

'What am I looking for?'

'The Chronicle of Brother Petrus.'

Chapter 22

Although the sea mist of the day before had cleared, there was still a leaden feel in the air. An anti cyclone was building somewhere across the Channel and, true to the climate's Entente Cordiale, the inundation would soon be shared with its English neighbours.

Moses Oradonte could smell the change in the upper atmosphere as the clouds rotated to generate lightning. If that brat, Angie, thought she had found the perfect hiding place above the high tide line, she could be in for a nasty surprise when flushed out by the storm's run-off from the cliffs. The charge in the air had been overpowering enough to raise the fur of the sniffer dog that had just given up and gone back to its kennels. Now it was up to a much rarer creature, a Fairdamon who could read the ways of an infant and not need to waste time searching drainage pipes or ditches. If Angie hadn't found a comfortable nook to hide in she would have emerged by now.

In the distance the child's mother, grandmother and Patsy gazed down at Moses as he strolled along the promenade, walking cane clicking in time to his leisurely pace.

Unlike Meg, who agonised over the way life treated her, Liz had an innate aptitude for living between the gaps opportunity presented. Having it made clear to her at school and by those who knew better that she was not destined to be one of life's achievers, the young woman had become one of life's survivors, rejecting the niceties of the society that had scorned her. Respect was a two-way street, and if no one would show her any, they needed to get out of the road.

Meg envied Liz her self-contained bubble, yet dreaded the day it would burst and splatter those nearest to her. If the worst did happen and the young mother eventually committed one misdemeanour too many and had to be removed from society, there was no way Meg could cope with her unlovely, unruly children - apart from Donnie who seemed impervious to the contamination of bad behaviour. How does anyone admit that they detest their own flesh and blood? So she took refuge in gin, cigarettes, bingo, and the occasional trip to the garden centre with Patsy, the only one who knew that Meg's frustration was born out of an intelligence no one would acknowledge when she was young. If it hadn't been for that, the woman could have made something of herself instead of helping to spawn yet another of life's losers.

Liz had never been able to cope with prolonged silence and assumed that when others were quiet it was because they were waiting for someone to speak.

She broke the brittle contemplation of the older women with a typical inanity, 'You sure your friend's that good, Patsy? He don't seem that sure where to look.'

'Don't be so bloody ungrateful!' snapped Meg. 'If the police and coastguard couldn't find her, he could be your last chance.'

Patsy understood all too well why her employer wanted Angie's family kept well away from him and said nothing.

Far below, Moses Oradonte's keen olfactory senses detected an unlikely sweet aroma mingling with the faint stench of decomposing seaweed. A sea worn plank moved slightly. These remote beach huts had been boarded up for years since the cliff above became unstable. The searchers didn't bother with them as even a grown man with a crowbar would have had difficulty breaking into one. So why could Moses detect the acidic sweetness of pear drops? Those before him had been looking for a panic stricken infant, not a calculating child determined to revel in the world's attention.

Moses struck the secure looking plank with his cane. It fell from the nail propping it up to swing down and leave a child-sized gap.

'You can come out now Angie. The game is over.'

But it would take more than sitting alone in pitch darkness for over ten hours to faze this little angel. The six-year-old's suppression of extreme discomfort was unnatural; even an adult with their sights set on an endurance trophy would not have had the determination.

'Go away!'

'You know I can not do that Angie.'

'Tell those cows I'm not going back!'

The exertion of dealing with irrational petulance brought back the pain his last injection should have been holding at bay. 'Very well, you little minx, stay there and see how long you can survive on a Diet Pepsi and packet of boiled sweets.'

Moses started to walk away.

Angie emerged like a furious little ferret that had been ejected from the burrow of a murderous rabbit. Her hair was tangled and the pretty pink clip that had held it in place dangled on a strand of curls like a swatted butterfly.

Moses tried to suppress his amusement at the ridiculous appearance of the dishevelled fairy, but this six-year-old could detect ridicule from the other side of the playground. How dare this strange man presume to interfere with the mischief of a superior being? Who did he think he was, with his carved, gold-tipped cane, immaculate clothes and clear, penetrating gaze that could outstare a cat?

Moses could usually discern an element of sensibility in the most disorganised of personalities, but not in Angie. He could only assume that the child was the product of a long line of self-interested souls who had survived at the expense of others for so long it had become written into the genes.

He had barely gone six paces when her shrill voice shrieked, 'Wait!'

He turned. 'Why? You obviously do not want to be found.'

'You can't leave me here.'

'You are free to leave and join your mother any time you please. I said I would find you, not drag you back kicking and screaming.'

'Nobody else could find me. How did you?'

'Pear drops and stale urine. It is quite disgusting.'

'I'll tell my mum what you said!'

Thankfully Liz and Meg realised that Moses had found Angie and were hurtling down the steps to the promenade, followed not too enthusiastically by Patsy. So, cane clicking out his indifference, her rescuer continued to walk away, confident that Wendy would be waiting in the car with an ampoule of morphine.

Chapter 23

Most seminars Dr Duncan Parfait was invited to speak at usually developed into lively debates about life originating on Mars and whether the lost continent of Atlantis sank beneath the Atlantic or North Sea. Not to mention "How could the great man be so sure that no antediluvian civilisation with technology equalling that of the present day never existed?" Duncan would then spend the rest of the evening patiently explaining that Mars, had it fostered life, would not have sustained a liveable environment long enough for any species to evolve technology capable of reaching Earth; Atlantis had probably been what is now called Santorini, which was devastated by a volcanic eruption back in the mists of time and given the apparent sophistication of these islanders it probably did seem more like a continent in the ancient world (or even Dogger Land, submerged under the North Sea - the people there not so sophisticated). And, if ancient populations had such remarkable technology, why didn't they use it to survive the last Ice Age? Then he would sit back, trying not to look smug, obliged to listen to all the carefully worked out responses to counter his authoritative explanations. The archaeologist could only marvel at the ingenuity of the Internet conspiracy theories that poured forth. At least it was gratifying to know that these, mostly, young people were paying attention to something more imaginative than war games. It could have been worse: the evolutionists he knew had to contend with creationists who believed in lynching heretics and shooting anyone working at abortion clinics.

All the same, by the time his latest seminar was wound up and the chairperson had thanked him for such a stimulating discussion, all Duncan wanted to do was crawl away to the Olive Grove and down several pints with Rolf Baker. The Rat and Compass was too harsh an environment to nurse an ego so tender from an evening of ridicule, even if it only came from the delusional. His researcher was the only one to subscribe to the antediluvian civilisation theory without Duncan feeling compelled to batter down his argument. Rolf was too knowledgeable to have his point of view dismissed and, knowing all the potholes in that road, could outmanoeuvre Duncan at every turn. So there was an amiable stand-off, neither mentioning antediluvian civilisations unless the other

72

did. And, after all, the researcher had provided most of the material on which he based his last book to discredit the theory.

However immaculate and with an ambience of the Mediterranean, the Olive Grove could never quite dispel the aroma of beer and crisps which the less adventurous of the customers insisted on. Here, the proprietor counted on his clientele, once inebriated, being malleable enough to consume a healthy option. Where other licensed houses served mash and mushy peas, Mario had the urge to mix pasta with everything, from tuna to chickpeas, which added an element of predictability to the meal of the day. Rolf much preferred the basic comfort of the Rat and Compass where you could spell what was on the plate. The local colour there came in all shades, including black and blue, but he could appreciate that the innately unpretentious Duncan was entitled to frequent an eatery that leaned, slightly, towards his celebrity status when his self-confidence needed a little massaging.

The researcher was an intense, intelligent young man whose thin, ginger appearance contrasted remarkably with Duncan Parfait's dark, full features that tended towards plumpness. The archaeologist was reluctant to admit just how much he depended on his young techno-savvy assistant with access to satellite operations that must have been subject to the Secrets Act. So when, after he had downed several beers, Rolf announced that he intended to give up archaeology and a find a "real" job, Duncan felt abandoned and almost on the verge of panic. That probably had more to do with inebriation, though the offer to double his researcher's pay wasn't.

To stop his benefactor from bursting into tears, Rolf agreed to reconsider his decision after talking it over with his partner, Charmian, who brought in the main wage. He had never seen Duncan this emotional and assumed he had either had a row with Carol - very unlikely: they either sulked or verbally battered each other with insults until one of them fell asleep - or he was hitting the male menopause and found the world becoming a more complicated place.

Not feeling too clever at breaking the news at that moment, Rolf finished his orange juice and drove Duncan home.

The strange empathy she shared with her partner had told Carol to wait in the mews for his arrival. The last time he came home inebriated, he had woken the businessman in the ground floor apartment, who threatened to have them evicted. Being more familiar with their tenancy conditions, Carol was all too aware he could have done it, and she had no intention of moving to Kings Cross, however convenient St Pancras and the Eurostar may have been.

Chapter 24

The balcony of Meg's council flat ran the full length of the lounge and kitchen combined. Standing on a plastic chair it was possible to see France. Even without it, through the gap between the derelict warehouse and terrace opposite, container ships were visible, plying the far side of the Channel like angular slugs crawling along a grey stone wall.

The springs in the velour settee had all but been destroyed by the children using it as a trampoline, and sticky fingers had made the TV remote virtually inoperable. Laundry hung from a clothes horse too large for the kitchen, plus every available nook that would accept a coat hanger. Meg's only break from the chaos that had overtaken her life was a trip to a supermarket or stroll along the seafront with Donnie, Liz's sweet-natured youngest. Unaccountably, the infant had never shown any urge to leap from his pram and chase pigeons or hurl pebbles at herring gulls. Meg often wished she had known his father, even at the risk of him feeling impelled to rescue the child from its inadequate mother.

Meg wished that she could be free of it all as Troy attempted to smash his toy tank to smithereens against the kitchen table, almost drowning out the sound of the washing machine's misaligned drum as it painfully skirled into final spin mode. She couldn't deal with the din any longer and went out onto the balcony to smoke a cigarette and watch the crows outmanoeuvring herring gulls for edible detritus and, in the far distance, huge ferries conveying the more fortunate to France.

'If you don't stop doing that Troy, I'll clout you!' she heard Liz scream from the kitchen. That was the well-worn threat she still used before managing to extend her vocabulary at a free evening class. It always came out when she was at the end of her tether and Meg didn't want to be in the same room when that snapped. Her best china teapot had ended up in pieces the last time it happened.

The dull thud of plastic against wood carried on. At least the washing machine had finished its cycle and screeched painfully to a halt. That was another thing Meg would be expected to fork out for when the bearings totally went. She briefly entertained the idea of anonymously reporting herself to the council for allowing Liz and her children to live in the flat so they would be obliged to find them accommodation, even though she ran the risk of being put out on the street without the hope of even a sheltered shoebox in the roughest end of town. At least here she had a view, and easy access to the shops and NHS drop-in centre.

The skirling of the washing machine was replaced by the high-pitched screech of Angie. 'I told you I wanted to wear that dress to Cindy's party, Mum! It won't be dry now!'

'It was filthy, you silly little cow! I ain't going to let any kid of mine turn up to some posh cow's house looking like a dish cloth!'

The child's tone changed to overweening smugness no six-year-old should have been mercenary enough to manage. 'But I need to look nice. They will expect me to tell them all about how I was rescued.'

'I bet they will - Will you stop doing that Troy!'

There was the sound of a child receiving a hefty smack round the head, followed by a howl of pain and rage, then clatter as the toy tank was hurled against Meg's new saucepan cupboard door.

Sometimes destitution had its appeal.

'Anyway,' Angie's self-interested whine went on, 'they won't believe it when I tell him how that strange man really found me.'

That had Meg listening intently.

'So how did he find you?' Liz asked offhandedly.

'By sense of smell.'

'Don't be so bloody daft!'

'It's true!'

'How could he have found you by sense of smell?'

'He said I smelt of pear drops... and he said I'd wet my knickers - but that wasn't true!'

Liz fell silent. Angie certainly had wet her knickers and Meg was pretty sure no respectable man in his right mind would have got close enough to the despicable child to smell that.

Meg took a deep drag on her cigarette. So that was why Patsy was so convinced Moses could find Angie. She always nursed the suspicion that there was an element of truth in the rumours that there was something supernatural about the man.

Domestic tornado over, baby Donnie returned his attention to the mobile in his pram and contentedly counted its coloured stars.

Chapter 25

Carol picked up the package marked "very fragile" and shook it a little too vigorously. Given the care with which it had been wrapped, insured for an astounding sum, and delivered by special courier, she had to know what was inside it. Unfortunately, one of the few house rules she shared with Duncan was only opening each other's post unless with permission or if odd substances were leaching through the wrapping. It would be an hour before he returned from the discussion about a new cable documentary and Carol was due at to give lecture in 30 minutes. By the time she returned the mystery inside the package would have been examined, sampled, catalogued, and no doubt sent on to another archaeologist for a second opinion.

The professor of economics wasn't so obsessed about the relics of the ancient world as her partner, though she did like to know when an interesting artefact turned up. It sent a shiver down her spine to touch something crafted by hands that had survived in a pocket of civilisation the ice sheets hadn't pushed into oblivion. In comparison, monetary matters of the recent past seemed dry; more to do with acquisition than achievement.

Picking up her briefcase and umbrella, Carol cast the mysterious package a resentful glance before reluctantly leaving to tutor ambitious, greedy youth in the ways of monetarism. For someone with socialist tendencies, the economist often wondered why she hadn't become an archaeologist instead; at least that would have qualified her to open the really interesting parcels.

Hot, bothered, and his easy-going disposition overwhelmed by the frustration of attempting to persuade a television producer that every episode from the past did not need to be simplistically dramatised

77

for the viewer to comprehend it, Duncan Parfait at last returned to the apartment. He made straight for the kettle. It was only the note, "I want to see this, Sugar Plum!" hastily scrawled in eyeliner on the parcel that drew his attention to the package before boiling water could meet teabag.

As the usually meticulous handwriting of Carol's had been reduced to such an unseemly scrawl, it must have contained a rare and extraordinary item to excite her interest. Duncan had no idea how she could tell the importance of something inside a sealed box. She was seldom wrong.

Before opening the parcel he circled it, stirring his mug of tea and examining the address label. Enough care had been taken over the wrapping to suggest that it had been sent by a museum or history faculty on the other side of the planet. But the return address was not foreign and other archaeologists usually contacted him first, at least emailing details of the artefact they were consulting him about. Carol was right yet again; there was something inexplicable about the object inside this parcel.

Duncan carefully split the tape with a sharp blade and lifted the outer layer away in one piece to find the precious sample cradled in a strong plywood box and swaddled in bubble wrap. The archaeologist was apprehensive about pulling it from its cardboard carton without knowing its fragility first. Then curiosity overcame caution. Dusting off the polystyrene beads adding yet another layer of protection, he gingerly removed the tissue from a strange statuette. It was of a long-limbed biped - not quite human - with straight, thoughtful features and halo of hair cascading about what appeared to be wings; or was it a cloak? The staff it clutch suggested authority, and the corona created by curled horns indicated a godlike status. But it was unlikely this creature had ever sat in the clouds dispensing justice. She was more probably the representation of a practical legal system that knew which way up to suspend any unlucky, or fortunate, plaintiff - a mysterious counterpart of the Egyptian Mayet. The ancient relic was crafted in a wood Duncan did not recognise. Despite being exquisitely tooled, the character it depicted came from no culture or mythology he had knowledge of, and he was familiar with most of them.

The card tucked inside the box gave nothing away. "Please examine this artefact, and then contact me if you find it of interest. If you do not, I will arrange for it to be collected."

Return the enigmatic piece without finding out what it was first? No chance! Dr Duncan Parfait's conclusion was going to be based on scientific investigation.

While waiting for those results, the archaeologist might let his imagination run riot a little but, given his reputation for integrity, hoped they would produce a conclusion profound enough to write a paper on, if not another book. Given his problems with the cable companies, and television producers in general, Duncan would have much preferred to invest his energies in another writing project and not have to deal with executives who were more interested in advertising potential than the historical archaeology it was sandwiched between.

He put on examination gloves, unwrapped a sample phial, and clinically removed a splinter from the base of the ancient wood where not even its secretive owner would have noticed.

Chapter 26

Initially Lottie felt as though she had entered the relaxed atmosphere of the Welcome Trust Library. This soon turned to bemusement when the reception desk directed her up several flights of stairs. From there she made her way through a labyrinth of corridors to a bland panelled door designated "archives" with a strip of embossed tape.

As she pressed the buzzer, Dr Freeman expected to encounter Rumpelstiltskin in a foul mood because he had been interrupted counting gold in his pokey little garret. Fortunately the door was opened by a moon-faced man in his early 40s. Though his expression was as bland and unassuming as the door, it nevertheless had a welcome twinkle of intelligence that suggested he was grateful for company. Isolated in his extraordinary eyrie of archives equipped with every electronic device conceivable to deal with enquiries, he only needed the one agile assistant to scale the heights where rare, seldom consulted, documents were stored.

'Mr Chapman of Chapman, Chapman and Son said you might help me.'

With an old-world flourish, the librarian invited her into the maze of high walls lined with volumes. The core collection was huge: whoever bequeathed it must have been a millionaire polymath.

There was the creak of ladders at the far end of the main room as his assistant climbed to the high ceiling to add yet another file box to an overloaded shelf. The long gallery above contained so many books it seemed incredible that the thin, cast-iron, columns could support them. Apparently this librarian believed that nothing, whether local history or esoteric tome, in his emporium would have had the bad manners to fall and to cause any scholar mortal harm. This was the domain of benign knowledge where the brutalities of the outside world did not apply. All the same, the doctor's medical instincts were automatically calculating the trauma that could be caused by some of the heavy Victorian reference books before realising that the librarian was waiting patiently to know her business. He was evidently used to visitors being taken aback when first entering his world as though it was academia's version of the Tardis, grateful he never had to contend with the exclamation, 'It's bigger on the inside!' Although, to all appearances, it must have been - there was little in the narrow corridor outside to suggest it was anything other than a broom cupboard.

'My name is Dr. Lottie Freeman.'

'Good morning, Dr Freeman. My name is Timothy Murdoch. How may I help you?'

Lottie was wrong-footed by the man's total lack of suspicion about someone he had never met before and involuntarily blurted out, 'I understand you have a copy of the Chronicle of Brother Petrus?'

'There is only one in existence,' he announced proudly as though someone had at last acknowledged the loving care lavished on an ancient relative. He beckoned Lottie to follow him through several stacks containing books with shabby bindings faded by handling and age. At the end of one was a small room containing glass fronted cabinets. Inside them flimsy pamphlets in perspex covers jostled with hefty tomes, some still with the links on their spines that had once chained them to their original shelves.

The librarian unlocked one of the cabinets filled with mediaeval volumes and other ancient parchments. He took out a plain, modern document folder and handed it to Lottie before reaching for a large, faded, leather bound book which he brought out into the main library where it was reverentially placed on a stand.

'Well, this is the Chronicle. It doesn't get out much, probably because it is in mediaeval Latin. Fortunately a previous librarian indexed many of our ancient manuscripts to prevent unnecessary handling.' He indicated the folder she held. 'What reference were you interested in?'

'The Companions of Urial.'

Timothy Murdoch's face fell as though he had found a misspelling in the Oxford English dictionary. 'Oh dear.'

'Oh dear?'

'The German secret service believed that they were

superhuman, you know.'

'What did they have to do with the Companions of Urial?'

'It's a strange story.'

'They did exist though?'

'Bizarre ideas, the Nazis had. Himmler possessed delusions about Aryans being evolved from cosmic ice crystals.'

'But the Companions of Urial did exist?'

'According to Brother Petrus, though that was not their true name. He created this myth about the Companions to conceal their real identity from the Church in case his Chronicle fell into the wrong hands. Everything about them was so much like a fairytale I doubt that the heretic hunters would have believed it anyway. The Third Reich, several centuries later, certainly did.'

Lottie at last sensed that she was getting somewhere. 'So you know something about them?'

'Oh yes.' He lowered his voice. 'I shouldn't. But I didn't sign the Official Secrets Act.'

'So our Secret Service was interested in them as well?'

'Oh yes.' The librarian went to another locked cabinet. 'In here we keep material for scholars studying ancient sexual mores and police investigators looking into satanic cults... and one or two old top-secret documents acquired nefariously from the files of MI5. The glue on some of the seals became very brittle, you know.'

Lottie smiled; it was gratifying to know that she wasn't the only one, when confronted by an envelope marked "secret", immediately opened it.

Timothy Murdoch pulled a folded map from a manila envelope and let it fall open on the table.

Lottie quickly looked it over. 'Fairdamon?'

'The so-called Companions of Urial. They lived in a secret walled town. Unable to photocopy it for you, I'm afraid.'

But Lottie was already jotting down any landmarks she could identify from the faded print. 'It's all right. I haven't seen a thing.'

Gratified that his visitor had enough discretion not to pull out a smartphone and start taking snaps, he waited for her pen to stop furiously scribbling notes then re-folded the map and returned it to the envelope. There was a self-satisfied flourish to the way he did it, which suggested such little episodes justified his cloistered existence.

Timothy Murdoch escorted her out with the same old-world charm with which he had invited her in. Once the door in that narrow corridor was closed, it was possible to believe that she had just been inside some archaic, alternative dimension.

Until then, Lottie had regarded the curiosity over her father's death as a legitimate interest. Even the younger Mr Chapman's dire warnings about him being a traitor and the explosion for which MI5 still apparently kept a file open hadn't come as any great surprise; that was all in the past with a million and other dirty secrets. But Fairdamon actually existed and the librarian's frisson of excitement at her interest smattered of something even deeper and darker.

There was only one way to get to the bottom of this mystery, whether Fred approved or not.

Chapter 27

As the automatic glass doors of the local newspaper office slid aside, Liz desperately hoped that she hadn't overdone the makeup or that her skirt was too skimpy. There was no guarantee that she would be meeting a male reporter, and she needed to present herself as a responsible parent, not an off-duty pole dancer. Liz should have told Meg before giving in to Angie's whingeing about appearing in the newspaper, but knew only too well what her response would have been to that. It had been enough persuading her to look after the children for an hour.

As she stepped into the intimidating glass foyer filled with plants that seemed uncomfortably carnivorous, Liz experienced an inexplicable surge of commonsense. Before she could spin round on her dangerously high heels and flee, the ridiculous fairy that had guided her there ensured that she was already standing at the reception desk, too late to change her mind. Then another fairy compounded her quandary by offering an unlikely helping hand.

'Hi Liz. How are you doing?'

She couldn't back out now. 'Hi Jan. I didn't know that you worked here?'

The plump, attractive woman behind the glass desk wore a surprised and, almost, friendly smile. From the beautifully manufactured welcome presented to all visitors, regardless of naiveté or criminal record, Liz was too self-consumed to appreciate she was actually something of an embarrassment. Angie may have only been six, but her antics had brought the local newspaper enough dubious copy for all its employees to be forewarned.

'I haven't seen you, Liz, since...'

Liz could remember well enough. 'School reunion, about four years ago.'

Jan squirmed internally at the reminder. 'Of course.' She could recall some of it. After half the young women ended up paralytically drunk in the nearest pub, everything after the arrival of the police remained something of a blur. Only beating her head against the bar of the holding cell could have caused the bruises she found on her face the next morning - either that or the kerb had decided to retaliate on behalf of the gutter she apparently rolled into.

'What brings you here?' she asked brightly.

Liz moved in closer as though dishing dirt on a local criminal gang. 'A couple of days ago my Angie got lost along the front. We all thought she'd fallen into the sea

84

and got eaten by a shark, but this friend of a friend found 'er. She could've died, trapped in this derelict beach hut, if he hadn't. After all the search parties and dogs never found 'er, we don't know how he did it. My mum's friend thinks he's a mystic of some sort, but my Angie swears blind he did it by sense of smell.'

'You're kidding.'

After the police had recommended that the next story this family generated be headlined KIDS OF INADEQUATE MOTHER CAUSE TROUBLE AGAIN any reports on the missing Angie were dismissed as yet another waste of time. Yet there was something in this latest saga that sounded as though it could be worth a couple of lines. Liz didn't have the imagination to cook up the scenario of a local mystic finding her brat by sense of smell; she had received too many warnings about her daughter wasting police time to risk pushing the same boat out yet again.

Jan picked up her phone. 'Hi Jerry. Have something down here that might be interesting. Got the police report from two days ago? Coastguard looks for six year old... Yeeees... That one.'

Liz was too occupied riffling inside her bag for an invitation to the celebration party for Angie's safe return to notice the circumspect tone. She had quite a few spare ones; for some reason the coastguard and police were too busy to send anyone, so she pushed a couple in front of Jan.

Jan looked at the name on the invitation. 'His name is apparently, 'Moses Ora... donte,' she told Jerry.

Liz nodded. 'The party's for him.'

'Can we send anyone?' asked Jan. 'Sure, I'll tell her.' She looked up at Liz with that automatic smile. 'What time does the party start?'

'Two to three - there'll be wine and nibbles.'

Oh good, at least they'll be lunch, Jan thought to herself. 'Yes, of course. One of our reporters would be pleased to come and interview this gentleman.'

Interviewing the person who had found her wasn't

quite what Angie had in mind, but Liz understood enough to know it was the only way of getting the press to come.

Chapter 28

Carol was accustomed to not seeing Duncan for days on end when their busy schedules overlapped, but she wasn't used to him sitting silently in his cluttered study with the lights turned down as though about to hibernate. He no doubt would have slept for the coldest months of the year when his Polynesian genes insisted he was in the wrong hemisphere: this was not one of those occasions. The archaeologist's uncharacteristic lapse into Nordic gloom had more to do with the carbon dating results he and Rolf Baker had been poring over. It didn't occur to her that the mysterious package that had arrived over a week ago, and which had gone by the time she returned from her lecture, could have been responsible for his apparent seclusion. She just assumed that whatever was inside it had been forwarded on for another opinion.

Their house rules declared that neither could disturb the other when working/thinking/writing/or just having a professional sulk over some troublesome colleague or review.

However, pasta could only be kept warm for so long, and with silence instead of the strains of Bach or Jacques Loussier issuing from the study, she decided it was time to resolve the dilemma.

The door was ajar and Carol looked in.

Duncan was just visible in the gloom, wearing blue examination gloves and clutching a small statuette as though it was a bird that would fly off as soon his grip was loosened. He appeared to be in intellectual catatonic shock, as though just discovering proof of an ancient Martian civilisation under Stonehenge. Carol had never seen her imperturbable partner plunged into such an introspective state of mind. Should she disturb him? Commonsense said leave well alone, yet curiosity insisted on her right to know about the ancient wooden artefact he clutched, its strange curlicues and features picked out by the hallway light.

Then she realised that it must have been in the package which had so intrigued her. Not only was Carol determined to know what it was, if Duncan refused to leave his study she would be obliged to eat both plates of pasta and have to spend an hour jogging it off.

'I know you're there, Liverwort,' his deep voice rumbled.

'It's not liable to be anyone else, Dunkin' Donut.'

'Have you eaten my dinner yet?'

'I would have at least checked your pulse before doing that.'

'Snatch a dead man's meal, would you?'

Carol knew he was trying to distract her from the statuette, so she turned on the light. Only then did she notice the dried tear stains on his swarthy cheeks. Any artefact capable of eliciting that response from the great man must have at least been from the lost continent of Atlantis. 'Just what is that thing?'

Duncan gave his face an embarrassed wipe. 'Only the end of everything I've spent half a lifetime railing against.' He handed her several pages of carbon dating results.

As they weren't economic graphs, Carol couldn't make immediate sense of them, and then realised that this strange figurine predated known history by millennia. 'Oh Duncan, is it that bad?'

'God no!' His face lit up. 'It's glorious... Bloody glorious!'

Chapter 29

Moses had told him accepted invitations to gatherings of more than three people - if it all. By the time he realised that the celebratory party for Angie's safe return was attended by several of Meg's neighbours, the odd - very odd - relation, and many of Liz's acquaintances who looked as though they had spent the night sleeping in an underpass, it was too late. By the expression on Patsy's face, she had also expected a discreet gathering with tea and biscuits, not cans of light ale, a smokers' haze and, worst of all, local reporter.

It was too late to retreat and Moses gave a convulsive cough as his inconvenient height encountered the cigarette smoke clinging to the low ceiling of the flat.

'Open the windows Meg!' Patsy demanded furiously.

Meg guiltily dashed through the rowdy throng and threw open the balcony doors. 'All smokers outside please!' she ordered.

Liz, clutching a tray full of economy nibbles, glared angrily across the room at her.

Meg glowered back with a look that told the young mother she and her brood were on the verge of eviction. Until then it had barely registered with Meg that she had not only alienated her oldest friend, but allowed in a reporter who could let drop that she was breaking every rule of her council tenancy by allowing Liz and her children to live there. To make matters worse, the self-elected star of the party, Angie, came skipping in from her bedroom like a miniature prima donna expecting applause. At last able to wear her best frock, she danced to the centre of the room, twirling and glittering like a badly pivoted mirror ball.

The reporter dutifully pulled out her smartphone and took a few low resolution snaps of the spoilt brat before returning to her glass of cheap sherry and slice of even cheaper quiche. She was more interested in

Meg who was showing her real quarry to the armchair Patsy had moved into a corner, away from the party.

As soon as the ironic applause at Angie's entrance had died down, the six-year-old was no longer of interest and everyone went back to gossiping and drinking. This was not what was expected and, determined to remain the centre of attention, Angie ignored the warning glowers of Patsy and Meg to skip over to Moses who had just lowered himself painfully into the armchair.

'You're the strange man who found me, aren't you?' the six-year-old sweetly simpered to conceal her real antipathy to the person who had dared ruin her prank.

Moses gave a tight smile at the thinly disguised accusation, and said nothing.

'Go away Angie,' Meg told her granddaughter.

'Why?' The child demanded petulantly.

Patsy fixed the girl with a steely glare Meg had never seen on her easy going friend's face before. 'Because you might end up being planted out with the petunias.'

'You wouldn't dare!'

'And I'm pretty sure you wouldn't sprout pretty, pink sequins if I buried you deep enough.'

'I'll tell my mum what you said!'

'You do that, because I got a few things to say to your mum, you little madam,' Patsy growled.

At last Angie recognised the danger signs and backed away unsurely.

The reporter watched the interaction. At last something of interest seemed to be happening. Yes, there evidently was a story in this mysterious man being guarded so fiercely by two ageing furies like the infirm god of some underworld. She would have to wait until they moved away, but had subsisted on worse junk food in her travels. Mechanically tidy in neat suit and high heels, which were obviously uncomfortable, Janine had long since given up any aspiration to become a journalist for a national newspaper. Without ambition, there was no reason to be unscrupulous. She had met enough people in the throes of ecstasy or trauma to realise that life was more interesting than that and would never know how close she was coming to the scoop of a lifetime in encountering Moses. If her humanity hadn't intruded, it might have been Janine's for a little ruthless probing.

When Meg and Patsy were sure that most of the gathering was out of earshot or on the balcony they left to corner Liz in the kitchen. The reporter poured some still spring water into a tumbler and took it to Moses.

'You look dehydrated.'

He accepted the glass and sipped it carefully. 'Thank you.'

'My name's Janine. I'm from the Herald.' She pulled a stool over and sat a discreet distance away from him. 'You weren't expecting this were you?' His expression needed no words. 'Always in trouble of some sort, this family,' she explained, 'ever since the police were compelled to release the brat's mother for shoplifting. She claimed it was the only way she could feed her kids. Like idiots, our paper took the story up. Been trying to shake off the brood ever since. Remarkable how gullible us reporters can be for the sake of copy.'

Moses gave the smart, slightly world-weary woman a penetrating look. 'So why are you here?'

'Guess.'

'The man who finds lost children by sense of smell?'

'Did you?'

'Oh yes, much against my better judgement.'

'May I print it?'

'Would you if I said no?'

'Not up to me. The editor expects me to come back with something, preferably not a photo of that little brat in a pretty pink dress. If I write it up, I can make sure it doesn't include anything you object to.'

'So that means your editor would think up something sensational if it was left to him?'

'Definitely, it's in his genes.'

'If you do something for me.'

'Name it?'

A sudden clatter and a tirade of abuse were reverberating about the kitchen.

'Apart from chucking that cow off the balcony - orphaning her brats would probably make the national press,' she advised.

'It is not necessary. I just need help to discreetly leave here.'

Janine laughed. 'Nothing easier. The car's not a Porsche, but air-conditioned. Where do you want to go?'

'The viewing platform would provide the fresh air I need. We can talk there.'

She put her smartphone away. 'We'll agree what goes in the story after we've escaped. Don't think I'll bother to tell our hostess how much we enjoyed the champagne and canapés.'

Chapter 30

As he entered the apartment, Rolf immediately knew by the jumbled pile of printouts and scribbled notes that Duncan had been attempting his own research and probably left for the pub in frustration. This invariably ended up with him spending hours sorting the master's jottings into a sensible order before either could make sense of them.

Carol took an uncharacteristically wary glance about the hall before closing the door and returning to the laptop where she had been working a safe distance from Duncan's chaos. 'Hi, Mighty Mouse. How's Charmian doing?'

'She thinks she's pregnant... again.'

'Well keep on practising if she isn't. If it doesn't make perfect, it's always fun.'

In wordless enquiry Rolf indicated the papers strewn about the floor and over the coffee table.

'Highly secret project. Not meant to know anything

about it in case it blows my mind.'

'What about mine?'

'If it hasn't exploded by now, it never will do.'

'If it's so secret, why has he left it strewn all over the place?'

'Probably forgot what reality he was in and could only deal with it by hunting down alcohol or caffeine.'

'But I told him I'd be here.'

'Despite the chaotic exterior, Dunkin Donut can be pretty perceptive on some levels. He must know you've got bad news for him.'

'Don't I know it, but he's well aware I've got to make a decision now Charmian could really be expecting. I want to carry on, but can't expect her to keep working full-time.'

Carol saved the file she had completed, closed her laptop, put on lipstick and teased some stray hair into place. 'Stand back if you're allergic to hairspray.'

Rolf moved behind the settee as she momentarily disappeared in a fine haze of lung-numbing mist.

Carol sneezed, and then suggested, 'You need to part-time or temp, then you can drop in and work for the great man whenever he has another rush of theories to the head. He could never write his hefty tomes without you.'

'Judging by this mess, he's certainly going to need a researcher when he decides to tell someone what this one is about.'

'You live in the East End, don't you Rolf?' Carol asked without warning.

'Two minutes from Canary Wharf.'

'I'll ask if there's any work about. There's always something for the numerically and alphabetically capable in the glass wonderland. Degrees don't count for much these days if you aren't literate. If you're good enough you might get flexi hours.'

'Great, thanks a lot, Carol.'

'Only don't drop anything on Dunkin' Donut until I get back to you. I never know what to do with him when he starts blubbing.' Carol picked up her briefcase. 'Gotta go now. Help yourself to coffee and feel free to read secret documents.'

When she had gone, the temptation was too great. Rolf came from behind the settee when the mist of hairspray had safely dispersed and began collating the scattered paper.

It was some while before a logical pattern came together in the ancient maps, print-outs, photocopies, and carbon dating results. When it did, a prickle of excitement tickled his scalp like a swarm of inquisitive ants. This disorganised research was millennia away from Duncan's usual comfort zone, some of the references pre-dating his specialist period by thousands of years. The archaeologist had been augmenting his comprehensive knowledge with material from other disciplines: he seldom gathered a whole pile from such diverse fields on just one topic. Was the great man at last seriously looking into the plausibility of an antediluvian civilisation to unearth the archaeological equivalent of an alien spaceship?

Rolf had become so immersed in the unlikely possibility, he was oblivious of Duncan standing over him until the deep voice asked, 'Managed to work it out?'

The researcher looked up at the ridiculous Hawaiian shirt and Bermuda shorts. 'You haven't actually been out looking like that, have you?'

'Only to the Olive Grove for a cappuccino. Had to give you time to plough through everything.'

'God, you really have to find someone to do your filing.'

'No need - got you.'

The man was incorrigible. Even if his research papers were a mess and dress sense appalling, Duncan Parfait had perfect timing and knew how to manipulate. It was that talent, more than his prodigious ability, which made him such an accomplished presenter. No ego, cynicism, or sneering, just this remarkable honesty and charisma that shone through the TV screen that increased his waistline and allowed him to get away with anything.

Sometimes Rolf wanted to throttle the man. 'This is blackmail, you know,' he accused.

'She's not pregnant,' Duncan promised him.

'I'm not so sure this time.'

'Look, if I'm right, I'll let you adopt me.'

Rolf turned over the possibility of his Charmian falling for the Polynesian charm and slightly overweight, shambolic looks. If he was a woman, against all common sense, he would have probably found the man attractive.

The researcher put the papers he was studying on the coffee table. 'Okay then. What have you found?'

Duncan planted himself in the armchair opposite Rolf, his face alight with enthusiasm remarkable even for his all-encompassing interests.

"Oh my God!" thought Rolf, "He's either discovered absinthe or a flying saucer under Stonehenge."

Duncan seemed on the verge of confirming his suspicion. 'I've found something even you won't believe, Rolf.'

'Is it worth doubling my fees for?'

'I'll triple them.'

Yes, Rolf decided, he's definitely been at the green fairy.

Chapter 31

Lottie had visited her private patients in the oddest places; at the end of kilometre long drives leading to dilapidated mansions, subterranean apartments with Olympic-sized swimming pools, and penthouses with landscaped gardens in the clouds. None of the routes to reach those addresses compared to these overgrown back roads. Virtually every lane leading from them was sealed off by fading signs warning of some ancient hazard or other and the doctor occasionally expected security teams to come dashing out and demand what she was doing there. Lottie wouldn't have been able to answer because she wasn't too sure herself. This must have been her misreading of the map she had hastily jotted down. The car's satnav refused to recognize landmarks and directed her to mediaeval roads that should no longer exist.

It wasn't until the rotting sign welcoming visitors to Greenbridge Village came into view that it transpired this was the correct route after all.

The first evidence of human habitation was a derelict railway station, and overgrown track which disappeared into a tangle of woodland, and then the occasional terrace along a potholed high street. Driveways from the overgrown village green led to much larger houses with ancient ornamental chimney stacks looming above the roofs of artisans' cottages.

This had once been a prosperous community with the squirely hierarchy typical of county manors. Now there wasn't even a blacksmith to shoe the occupants of a donkey sanctuary, or evidence of any livestock - even the ubiquitous RSPCA charity shop. This was a creepy community deep in the countryside which had detached itself so completely from the rest of Nature even the pigeons thought twice about roosting in the roofs of derelict houses. Something cataclysmic in its past had pulled the comfortable community rug from under the village and, after seeing what was beneath it, never bothered to put it back.

Greenbridge now had few residents. On the way to nowhere, this was hardly second home territory. By the lack of estate agent boards, that mysterious blight had made it an anathema to them as well. Any vehicles which had not been turned into chicken coups or allowed to rust away could have barely scraped through their last MOT and the occasional inhabitant viewed her expensive car with hostility. Lottie would have carried on driving if she hadn't needed further directions to avoid disappearing into this unmappable realm her satnav refused to recognise.

There was the incongruous sign of a post office amongst some derelict shops on the other side of the unkept village green. The bright, round, red sign announced that this near dead community still had a heartbeat after all.

Lottie stopped the car and went into the shop to take its pulse.

The low ceiling from which wind chimes and ancient Christmas decorations hung made it feel like a doll's house designed by a colour-blind magpie. The cluttered shelves of groceries were obviously cleaned regularly, but this could not eradicate the musty smell as they radiated away into the depths of a recess that had probably once been another room. Some products were so old, the packets containing them were probably collectable, which would have been the only reason anyone would have bought them. At least the baked beans and cereals within reach appeared to be still within their sell-by dates. The building, judging by the small windows and dangerously low beams was old and no doubt had a rudimentary cellar for foundations; the only corner remotely modern being the brightly lit post office counter plastered with out of date posters and faded customer postcards advertising kittens and odd job services.

The shop's elderly proprietor sat in a wicker chair by the grocery counter, under the shelves of dry goods. A small glass fronted fridge mumbled erratically in the corner as it tried to keep cans of fizzy drinks chilled; a rack of local vegetables seemed to be the liveliest things there.

'Good morning,' Lottie announced in her professional voice, knowing she was bound to be ignored if she sounded too civil.

The proprietor recognised the medical tone which made him recall his varicose veins and he immediately looked up.

'I need directions,' Lottie went on before he had chance to decide how to react, 'and a top up for the mobile.'

A flicker of terror crept into the old man's eyes at the mention of technology. 'The old woman does the post office. She keeps them things behind there.' He indicated the brightly lit counter with his thumb.

He was bald, blotchy and too well fed, and no doubt the reason why his elderly wife needed to lie down after taking delivery of stock and filling shelves. Type 2 diabetes and pulmonary embolism just round the corner here, Lottie thought to herself, if he doesn't have a stroke first.

'Not to worry, I've got a couple of hours left on it. I'll have a bottle of spring water instead.' Lottie could see the old fellow would resent having to leave his wicker chair for such a miniscule sale, so she reached into the fridge and pulled a bottle out.

'That's a pound, missus.'

It wasn't too high a price to pay for directions so Lottie promptly handed it over.

'Where you going then?'

'Fairdamon.'

The expression on the proprietor's face changed so dramatically Lottie almost admitted that she was a doctor, but didn't want to encourage the old man to have his heart attack then and there for the sake of convenience.

'That's an odd place to want to go to?' he said disapprovingly.

'How come?'

'Odd bleeders used to live there at one time. Before the last War, that was.'

'Odd? How come?'

'Didn't look like other folk, kept themselves to themselves. Some said they had supernatural powers.'

Lottie tried not to sound too interested to keep him talking. 'You don't say?'

It worked and the old man switched into local

gossip mode. 'One lad I used to bring boiled sweets for when the train ran through here - they didn't go anywhere unless it was on a train in their own private compartment - he could smell whether my old dad had them in from the other end of the village.'

The boiled sweets Lottie could remember from her childhood did have that effect on children, though usually not from half a mile away. 'Why did they leave?'

The proprietor suddenly realised that he was saying too much and became defensive. 'Cleared out they were. Min of Ag - or whatever they were called then - said it was foot and mouth or some such thing. Couldn't afford to deal with an outbreak of anything with war looming, so just sealed the place off.'

'The Fairdamons?'

'Who knows?' He shrugged and returned to his newspaper. 'Odd lot they were...'

'Can you give me directions?'

'Can't understand why anyone would want to go there.'

'I'm researching abandoned towns for a report, a sort of directory to prevent illegal archaeological digs,' Lottie lied.

He seemed relieved. 'I suppose that's all right then. It's not as though anyone's liable to get in there.'

'Why not?'

'It's been walled off since the War.'

'Walled off?'

'Anthrax, they said.'

'As well as foot and mouth?'

The old man had been wrong-footed and wasn't going to give any more away.

'Okay,' Lottie told him, 'in that case I won't try.'

'If you want to see the posters for yourself, the town's straight on past the memorial and second on the right. Scratch the paintwork on your nice new car taking that road, though.'

'One or two brambles on the way here got in there

98

first. Don't get many visitors, do you?'

'That's the way we like it.'

Lottie had no doubt about that. 'Thanks a lot. Perhaps I'll pop in for a top up on the way back - when does the counter open?'

'When old Doug Harris wants his pension, or the old girl's finished her nap. Give it an hour.'

Lottie left with her pointless bottle of spring water. As soon as she had driven off, the proprietor left the comfort of his wicker chair to go to a bakelite phone concealed behind some ancient biscuit tins. 'Sorry about this old girl,' he muttered to himself, 'but if I don't tell them we could lose our licence.'

He leafed through a shabby notebook hanging above it and shakily dialled a number.

Chapter 32

Dr Duncan Parfait looked apprehensively at the fantastic beasts guarding the wrought iron gate. Beyond it immaculately manicured hedges bordering a chequered pavement in the large front garden. At the centre of each pale, pink square sat a terracotta pot; not filled with flowers, but neatly clipped bay trees. The man who owned this house was either colour blind or a control freak.

The archaeologist was tempted to leave the parcel he carried on the front step, ring the bell, and make off. And he might well have done if a small, neatly dressed woman hadn't opened the front door and beckoned him inside before he had the chance.

Surprisingly, the house was filled with light and colour, much of it reflected from mirrors and through Art Nouveau stained glass, and Wendy's Far Eastern elegance, made the dreamlike space of reflection and luminosity complete. To his archaeologist's eye the exquisite glass vases and Tiffany lamp shades were all genuine.

Duncan was a seasoned performer, practised at dealing with audiences who wanted the Universe to be more mysterious, yet had to admit he was already intimidated. Some demon of insecurity was whispering that the magician who owned this house would easily persuade him away from the precious absolutes to which he still clung, despite tangible evidence that was undermining them. He was standing at the summit of an intellectual Eiger, about to be blown off by the breeze of an unfathomable and frightening alternative prospect.

Wendy waited patiently while the archaeologist dealt with his demons like a schoolboy just learning that Daleks not only existed, but could also levitate, before politely ushering him to the far side of the open plan hall and lounge. Compared to the rest of the decor there was nothing unusual or ornamental about a half-open door, which was oddly reassuring.

Wendy went in and invited Duncan to follow.

The study of Moses Oradonte was crammed with objets d'art, engravings, and books - shelf upon shelf of books. If everything hadn't been methodically arranged, Duncan might have recognised a kindred spirit. But the intricate design of the Persian carpet was too esoteric for the sensibilities of someone who believed Hawaiian shirts and Bermuda shorts to be the height of good taste. And the curtains half drawn across the French windows were shot silk, their pale, plum-coloured sheen complementing the dark green of the garden outside. Once he had noticed that, the archaeologist almost became transfixed by the velvet moss that covered its seats, ground and walls. It took some effort to haul his attention back to the matter in hand, the parcel he was clutching like a child with a pet puppy.

The tall man sitting at the desk rose and came forward to shake his hand as though he only touched other people when it could not be avoided. It was difficult to tell whether Moses Oradonte was relieved that the archaeologist had decided to accept his invitation, or apprehensive at the possible reaction to what he was about to tell him. Duncan was well aware that he was on the verge of learning something that would finally demolish his world view, and wished that this intellectual of the iceberg persuasion would at least give some indication he appreciated that. Hotheads and the delusional were easily dealt with, but cool customers usually put forward better arguments.

Wendy left and discreetly closed the door after her.

'Please take a seat, Dr Parfait.'

Duncan sat obediently, wondering at the shelves of books that would not have been out of place in the Bodleian library, and trying to get the measure of the man who had inherited them; he was convinced that many of them were too valuable to offer at auction.

Duncan held his breath in anticipation as Moses went to a plan drawer and took out a replica map. The archaeologist was perversely relieved to at last be encountering something that was not the genuine article.

As though reading his thoughts, Moses explained, 'The original is far too fragile to handle.'

There was something about the map that made Duncan want to reach out and take it, but the document was laid out on the desk instead.

'Before Wendy brings us some coffee, you no doubt need to ask me a question?'

Duncan took the ancient, wood statuette from the parcel, unwrapped it, and placed it next to the map. 'Where did this come from?'

'It came from a long, long, while ago, as your investigations have no doubt proved.'

'Who made it?'

'That is more complicated.'

'You can't tell me?'

'Not at the moment. Though you are aware of the implications, I appreciate that you will need more proof.'

Duncan was disconcerted that the man could read him so well and demanded, 'Why choose to tell me?'

Moses sat down, the shadow of a smile crossing his saturnine features. 'Because I believe you can be trusted.'

Duncan wasn't sure whether to be flattered or not. He felt like a mouse being toyed with by an academically superior cat that played with its prey before putting it down with a devastating one-liner. 'Why is being trustworthy such an issue?'

'I need you to give me your word.'

At last a request that made the guest feel more like an equal.

'For what?'

'For letting you know the most unsettling truth human beings are ever likely to confront about their past.'

This is what the archaeologist had been anticipating, as much as it flew in the face of a lifetime spent shooting down other people's fantasies about the ancient world. However desperately he wanted to know the truth, he realised from experience that there was always a price to pay for each earthshaking revelation. 'What do you want me to give you my word about?'

'Your silence.'

Duncan's draw dropped at the prospect of this precious, soul-searching project going nowhere. Could any truth be so apocalyptic it is better kept secret?

'Until I am dead anyway,' Moses added.

Duncan tried not to look too relieved. Though the man was in his early 60s and seemed a little frail, he could live quite a few years yet. By that time Duncan could have descended into an alcoholic haze at having to sit on the greatest ever archaeological breakthrough, simply because he made a promise.

'I do not have that long to live now,' his host announced dispassionately.

Duncan's jaw dropped again; this time because he

had no idea what to say without the sympathy sounding too mercenary.

'By the time you and your able researcher have pieced together enough evidence for publication, I will not be here.'

This threw up an inevitable problem. 'If we need to excavate anything to prove something this profound it will take money, and no one sponsors a dig unless they have an idea what we are looking for. Whatever the purists claim, it always helps if there are sparkly and obscenely valuable artefacts at the bottom of the hole.'

'It is not necessary to dig for treasure, though you will need a ship in due course.' Moses at last handed Duncan the map. 'Most of the sites located on this are underwater. Those that are not have been eroded away or lay metres below major ports.'

Printed on the large sheet was an exact facsimile of a map so ancient the locations were indicated in a language more symbolic than script. Despite the variations in coastlines, the topography of an almost complete world was amazingly accurate, something that should have had not been possible before aircraft. The reproduction was fine enough to tell the archaeologist that the original sheet had been made from a finely crushed, cream fibre and the pigments had a wider spectrum than those that could have been derived from earth minerals and plants alone.

Although bursting with questions, Duncan satisfied himself with a professional, cursory glance, paddling on the shore of curiosity before risking his integrity to deeper waters. Whatever stance he assumed, he was convinced that the tall, taciturn enigma was still reading his mind.

He gave the map back to Moses, who rolled it and placed it in a document tube.

Moses handed it to Duncan. 'When you are satisfied that there is something worth excavating, I will show you the treasure.'

The effect on the archaeologist was electric. Not

only was the man about to undermine the convictions of every modern historian, he was offering treasure as well. He hoped that his face hadn't lit up like a metal-detecting amateur finding the proverbial golden horde. It was a wasted effort. It was apparent that Moses Oradonte could read others as easily as a wine menu.

There was a rap at the door and Wendy brought in a tray of coffee.

When she had gone Duncan warned Moses, 'Do you trust Rolf to keep quiet as well? You know I can't manage this without him?'

'Oh yes, he holds you in too high a regard to do otherwise.'

It was disconcerting that Moses knew that, yet secretly gratifying to have it confirmed. Duncan was unsure whether the young man's trust in his integrity was always warranted.

'You have an interesting time ahead of you, Dr Parfait, believe me.'

Duncan could do little else but sit like a schoolboy, prickles running up his spine, at being praised by the headmaster for something he hadn't yet achieved. He sipped his coffee and tried not to think about treasure.

Chapter 33

After Kath and Neville had spent many happy years together, memories of her old, mysterious lover faded. For Kath, Moses would always unobtrusively be there in the Art Deco stained glass of the front porch Neville had glazed and the moss that resolutely clung to the east facing side of his rockery. The main difference being that Moses' moss garden wasn't dotted with the star-like flowers of alpine plants.

The rundown bungalow in an acre of land they had bought at auction was now a chalet with extensions on every side, an orchard of Victoria plums, Cox's apples, Williams's pears, and a fig tree hell bent on undermining any foundations within reach. Sooner than dig up the fig tree, the enterprising Neville had sunk a wall to prevent its roots reaching the family home.

Once the children had left, their lovingly cherished real estate suddenly became a warren of vacant rooms with picture windows from where their offspring could once be watched at play. The early retirement that had enabled Neville to build this small empire now seemed empty and, to his surprise, he began to envy Kath her florist shop. Ever the pragmatist, he turned his gaze to that part of the grounds which would have been a wild flower meadow if it hadn't kept filling with brambles and nettles. He hired a rotovater, turned over the soil of this unholy end of God's acre, and put in foundations for the largest domestic greenhouse on that side of the Mersey. Then Neville started to propagate pot plants; hibiscus, calceolaria, streptocarpus, gloxinia, chrysanthemums, begonias, etc. - virtually everything Kath could sell in her shop, with enough surplus for small local supermarkets.

And, so the hole that had opened up when their children had moved out was filled with potting, pruning, and haggling over the price of cyclamen. Even the pointless picture windows were used to bring on tender rarities which usually had to be imported. Kath was surprised and gratified at how tough a bargainer her husband turned out to be, even with her.

Although the income ended up in the same flowerpot, the negotiations kept the mind sharp and sense of self-preservation keen. Neither of these Derby and Joans would end up in care, eking out a dwindling existence while the familial vultures gathered.

Just as life settled down to a steady pace, a letter arrived out of the blue.

Kath could still recognise the handwriting on the envelope after all these years and took a deep breath. She had reluctantly kept to her side of the agreement with Moses that they should never meet again. For him to contact her, it must have been important. Loath to open the envelope to find out how catastrophic, Kath took it to Neville who was pottering around in the greenhouse, teaching one of his work experience teenagers the mind-numbing art of separating seedlings. He saw his partner standing in the aisle of carnations ready to be cut, and wondered why they had never married, if only so he could have seen her in full, floral glory. Then he realised from his partner's expression that marriage vows were the last thing on her mind.

Kath handed Neville the envelope.

Without a word, he took a penknife from his pocket, slit it open, and gave the letter to Kath who silently read it. She handed it back and Neville perused the copperplate writing. During all the years they had been together, raising a family, Kath still experienced misgivings whenever the subject of Moses cropped up. Neville had never regarded her ex-lover as a threat, and was more inclined to wonder why she had left this mysterious, wealthy paragon for him. During his life furnishing and fitting out luxury yachts he had heard of stranger things happening at sea, though not usually for the good.

'Well, it seems a great way to spend a week,' he announced stoically. 'I'm sure the business can do without you for that long and there's enough potting on to keep my bunnies busy for the next fortnight.'

The teenager cast him an apprehensive glance which didn't register with his employer.

Kath daren't admit that she was reluctant to see Moses after so many years, unsure which one of them would be more appalled by the change in the other. 'Sheila expects one of us to babysit while she's away on that course.'

'That's not what these grandparents are for. She knows we're working.'

'She thought...'

'Sheila can afford a babysitter. She doesn't need us

to do it.'

Kath admired the mild Neville's tough stance, though knew what he really wished to say. 'You want to meet Moses, don't you?'

Neville couldn't deny it. 'Is that bad?'

'No, just a bit odd.'

'And he does make a point of wanting to meet me.'

That was a part which worried Kath most. What could the two ageing men have to discuss other than her? 'You are sure you want to do this?'

'This old flame of yours has a mature moss garden and it's worth risking the ire of our overindulged offspring to see something like that.'

'Yes, I suppose that means Patsy is still with him. I would like to meet her again.'

Chapter 34

As soon as Carol saw Rolf sitting on the lounge floor amongst so many satellite maps, she knew that Duncan's mysterious project had sprouted wings. Some of the locations appeared to be in the Mediterranean, so there was a least the chance to spend a couple of weeks scuba-diving in the Aegean. Duncan swam like a dog with a hernia despite his seafaring ancestry and was bound to need her expertise - assuming he ever admitted what he was looking for.

'Hi Carol. How's life?'

'Not as chaotic as yours by the look of it. What has the great man found?'

Rolf was obviously exasperated. 'I'm not sure. He just keeps muttering stuff about a piece of the spacecraft and a discovery profound enough to blow away the human misconception about its identity.'

Since social networking sites had allowed people to exist in their own safe, little compartments so they never needed to open the door of reality, Rolf had cherished the possibility that he could be in the vanguard of a major archaeological discovery which would shake up their little worlds. At worst, it could create yet another conspiracy theory for them to get worked up about.

Carol examined one of the infrared printouts. 'This is a military image. Boy, you must have some moles out there.'

Rolf shrugged. He wouldn't even admit to Duncan how he had built up his network of contacts, let alone name the relatives that had enabled him to do it.

Carol was suddenly aware of how empty the apartment seemed with only the presence of the quietly contained Rolf. 'So where is Dunkin' Donut?'

'Went up to the roof to think.'

Carol knew it was more likely he needed to make a phone call without being overheard. Given the secrets the two men kept from each other it was amazing how much they achieved together.

Closer examination of the image she held revealed the faint outline of ruins in the sea some distance from the Spanish coast. They would have been barely visible to someone more interested in military installations. The mathematician in Carol scrutinised every anomalous shadow in the, otherwise, bland ocean. With the help of a magnifying glass and strong light, she could just make out the boundaries of a large, submerged city; and then structures within it. The ruins were located in an area she knew well, yet were unknown to her scuba-diving companions. That something so vast on the seabed had escaped their attention was remarkable. Though it didn't explain Duncan's excitement over this particularly large, ancient city after he had helped excavate so many brought to light by infrared satellite imaging.

Then Carol understood. No inundation in recorded history could have accounted for the strange ruins so far from shore.

A prickle of excitement skittered over her scalp as the implication of their great age occurred to her. 'My

God...'

Rolf looked up. 'Now you can start to take a few good guesses as well.'

'This has to be impossible.'

'If the military hadn't been using infrared to pinpoint subs which were never there, we'd be none the wiser.'

'Are they aware of what's in these images?'

'Probably, but are hardly likely to admit that they've been spying on their allies.'

'I'm not surprised Duncan wants you to keep quiet about it - palaeoarchaeologists would soon be muscling in if they found out.'

Rolf cast her an intense glance. 'So please don't mention it to anyone else, Carol.'

She replaced the infrared image and held up her hands. 'Me undermine anything the great man is doing? I'm just glad he's been struck round the ear with the wet fish of revelation. His menopausal melancholy of dissatisfaction was beginning to get me down as well.'

Chapter 35

The proprietor of the village post office had not exaggerated the difficulty of getting to Fairdamon. Lottie had to negotiate a twisting, potholed road to reach it, only to find the deserted town enclosed by a high stone wall topped with broken glass and razor wire. The anthrax posters, although faded, still blazoned their dire warning as though the squirrels needed to be reminded.

Lottie drove on round the narrow perimeter road until noticing an ancient wooden door in a recess. It was virtually concealed by nettles and bracken and seemed to be the only way of getting in. She parked her car on the overgrown verge to allow the odd horse or cyclist to pass and then took some gardening gloves from the boot to pull away the nettles. The ancient padlock and chain had rusted together, but the wood they were secured to was rotten. Lottie went back to the car boot and took out a monkey wrench. She delivered the padlock several hefty blows and the bracket it was secured to fell away. The ancient door opened slightly. Through the gap it was possible to glimpse a haunted looking valley of overgrown fields and woodland.

Nothing had lived here for decades and the topography suggested the inhabitants had farmed vegetables and fruit instead of cattle. By the way plots of land had been divided up, and the number of orchards coming into fruit, the Fairdamons had been an agrarian society, probably vegetarian.

Given the length of time that had passed, the anthrax posters must have been redundant: the bacteria of the disease could not have survived in isolation for that long.

After the scouring her car's paintwork had received from the brambles and branches on the journey there, nothing much worse could happen to it, unless the badgers knew how to hotwire the ignition, so Lottie left it where it was and squeezed through the gate.

Primed to encounter the unexpected, the sight that met the visitor nevertheless made her stand and stare.

Fairdamon was no ordinary town. Its polished stone in the gently sloping valley reflected the sun's rays like a benign outgrowth of white quartz. At its centre there was a large colonnaded square - or what was once a square. It was difficult to make out from that vantage point.

The asymmetry of the domes, gables, and spires created a jigsaw which revealed Fairdamon's history. The lower, steeply pitched roofs were the most ancient, their ridges concave with age, the more modern rising magically from the confusion in confidently pirouetting steeples and cupolas.

Whatever the real reason the army had for

quarantining the town, it wasn't manoeuvres. The land had never been pockmarked by tanks and the only damage the buildings had suffered was from neglect.

Lottie fought her way through an overgrown track that wound down into Fairdamon and its exotic architecture with a bleached Aegean - almost Middle Eastern - ambience. As well as the balconies, decorative shutters, high gables and cupolas, there were towers that seemed to defy gravity and overhead walkways apparently suspended in the sky without tangible support which, after 70 years of dereliction must have been held up by cobwebs. Some streets were unexpectedly spacious and ablaze with rosebay willowherb and yellow corydalis.

The main thoroughfare led to a building ostentatious enough to be a town hall or library. As Lottie ascended its steps a cloud of dandelion seeds wafted up, some determinedly clinging to her crinkly hair, and the occasional pink clump of soapwort made colourful punctuations against the granite and white marble.

Lottie pushed the carved wooden door and it creaked open. Light from a domed roof flooded a spacious chamber. It had a huge span which had not been possible to recognise from outside because of the other buildings clustering about it like a baby marsupials attached to their mother. The metal ribs supporting the dome looked too fragile to bear its weight, shimmering like streamers soaring into the sky. Most of the ornamental reliefs entwining the ceiling's supporting pillars had survived the ravages of neglect while the eyes of fantastical animals peered from cornices of alabaster foliage.

No, this was not a town hall or library.

Although stripped of any fittings that might have provided a clue, the interior was unlikely to have accommodated tiers of seats or shelves. The cavernous space could have been a big top waiting for trapeze artists, though its cathedral silence was more suited for contemplation where thoughts could take their own acrobatic flights of fancy. The flapping of pigeons' wings broke the hush of centuries and unsettled the doctor who was more used to the shallow world of hypochondriacs and patients who couldn't deal with life. Perhaps she would come back when she reached her mid 80s and give it a go. Not wanting to contemplate the iniquities of ageing at that moment, she left silently and pulled the door to. The atmosphere outside was different, infused with ghostly traces of the bustling population that once inhabited Fairdamon. This had to be the enchanted kingdom after Sleeping Beauty pricked her finger on the spinning wheel. The compact, terraced dwellings with their carved porches and ornamental screens should have been occupied by dreamers waiting for a mythical prince to kiss the realm back into life.

Lottie would have stepped inside one of the homes if some indefinable feeling had not constrained her. Curiosity had to be satisfied with glances through windows where she could just make out rooms filled with furniture, like dolls' houses and tables laid with crystal ware catching the odd ray of sunlight as though waiting for the occupants to return. Yet the ceilings were high to accommodate tall inhabitants who were otherwise not obsessed with personal space. The lower rooms were probably only meant for one person. This seemed a good idea to a medical practitioner who had always believed that separating some families would have saved society a lot of grief. Here, it seemed they had worked out a long while ago that cohabiting was not natural for all people.

After meandering the narrow streets, alleyways and steps leading from the main thoroughfare for almost an hour, Lottie passed a semi-demolished terrace. Suddenly she found herself in the town's central square. The large space was surrounded by colonnade, quite gappy in places.

There had been a catastrophic explosion here.

What had once been Fairdamon's heart was now a vast crater.

Dr Lottie Freeman gazed into the deep, flooded crater with exasperated amazement. 'Anthrax, my arse!'

It was difficult to tell what had caused the destruction. It could hardly have been cosmic; the impact area was too exact and could have only been made by a weapon. Perhaps this mysterious community had a nuclear device long before the hydrogen bomb was a gleam in Oppenheimer's eye. At least it would explain why an already nervous War Office, on the eve of war, opted to evacuate Fairdamon and seal it off. The most surprising thing about it was how, given the Freedom of Information Act, this hadn't surfaced long ago. But then, if it had been so well covered up in the first place, who would have been sufficiently aware to insist it be made public?

At least Lottie now knew where her father and his Nazi followers met their Valhalla.

Mystery of a lifetime solved, she wasn't expecting to encounter another one, so wended her way round the crater to the most intact side of the colonnade. Stretching away on its sheltered wall was a continuous line of plaques listing what appeared to be deceased Fairdamons. The language on the oldest was incomprehensible, apart from the odd date. English had evidently taken over as the centuries passed.

This town was truly ancient if the plaques and circle of standing stones just visible on the far side of the valley were anything to go by. Having little knowledge of archaeology, Lottie would have said that Fairdamon stretched back before the Stone Age when there were no inscriptions let alone iron chisels to carve them. But those early symbols appeared to be far more complex than runic characters. How could such an advanced community have gone unnoticed by the amateur archaeologists who now swarmed legally, and illegally, over the countryside? This prehistoric

Portmeirion had managed to don a cloak of invisibility and dissolve into a rolling green wilderness walled off by the War Office and Ministry of Agriculture anthrax posters.

Lottie stood stock still for a moment, on the verge of believing that the Fairdamons whose names she was jotting down in her notebook had somehow overcome mortality. It was likely that the realities of other mere mortals had meant nothing to this strange community. Into her awareness crept a fancy that their essence was still there, watching and waiting. She felt caught in a benign web which would only release her when she understood what had illuminated their existence.

Not knowing why, Lottie felt impelled to brush the grime from a gold inscription commemorating one particular family she had overlooked before. Their name was no more unusual than all the others; but something persuaded her to add it to the list in her notebook.

Then cold reality returned with a shudder. What on earth was she doing in this decorative, dead town, writing down the names of its deceased? The mystery of her father's death was solved and that should have been enough.

Well aware that she was trespassing and not wanting the hassle of being investigated by MI5, Lottie resisted the urge to take incriminating snaps of Fairdamon on her smartphone, and silently left the dead to their perpetual slumber, hoping they would never be disturbed. The thought of the ghostly town being transformed into a golf course or vulgar theme park was too unsettling.

Chapter 36

The train journey from Central London had been straightforward but, before Duncan took a taxi to his final destination, the usually unflappable media presenter reluctantly gave into the need for liquid courage. He knew that there were no pubs in the vicinity of the house owned by the mysterious man he was calling on, so went into the nearest hotel lobby with a bar.

After swigging back two whiskies, he glanced at his watch, determined to be punctual for once in his professional life: this time it could matter more than any multimedia project costing millions.

Standing by an open window, Moses could detect the alcohol on his visitor's breath before he reached the front gate. He almost regretted that the man needed to pluck up courage to face him.

Wendy duly escorted the archaeologist into the lounge where Moses was gazing out at a sky so intensely blue angels must have been swimming in its ocean. He turned and offered his conflicted visitor a rare half smile of reassurance.

'Please take a seat.'

Duncan slumped into an armchair like an admonished basset hound. He looked up warily at the tall enigma when he asked, 'So, are you now persuaded?'

'Rolf is convinced I'm trying to conceal the find of the millennium from him.'

'Are you not?'

'He worked it out as soon as he matched the infrared satellite images to your map.'

'So you now both feel it imperative to dash off and excavate?'

'Of course we do, but made an agreement. I may like the odd tipple, overeat, and perform like a monkey on pogo stick when there's an audience, but I always keep my word.' The significance of his dilemma made

Duncan pause. 'Apart from that, it could take years to raise the funds to excavate any of those underwater sites.'

Moses sat in a high backed armchair facing the archaeologist and reminded him of a jade statuette of an enthroned Oriental monarch as he announced, There is no need to worry about that.'

Duncan cast a hopeful, inquiring look as though the king was about to make a judgement. 'No?'

'You will have all the capital you need, and more, in due course.'

The man must have been as rich as Croesus. 'How?'

'Your patience will be rewarded, I promise. In the meanwhile...'

'Yes?' Duncan asked expectantly.

'I will show you something that could never be recovered from a thousand excavations.'

This brought out in the archaeologist the Boy Scout greedy for another badge. 'You mean... there are more artefacts like the one you sent me?'

Moses gave that unreadable half smile in reply. 'It requires an appointment with the bank but, while you are here, I would like you to meet someone.' Moses pressed the button on an intercom. 'Wendy, could you persuade Patsy to allow Miss Kandy to come in for a moment?' He turned back to Duncan. 'Miss Kandy has a passion for petunias and pansies unusual for a solicitor with only a window box.'

'Solicitor?'

'In due course she will handle all my affairs, so it is better you meet her now.'

To Duncan, this could only mean one thing. Against all the odds, he actually liked Moses Oradonte and preferred not to think of him dying. On the other hand, he was desperate to gather together an excavating team and travel to exotic locations where the origins of human civilisation could at last be explained.

Moses could easily tell what he was thinking. 'There

116

were giants in those days...'

'What..?'

'Some human myths are based on ancient memories.'

The archaeologist was well aware of that, but could "giants" have really built the first civilisations?

Moses understood his silent scepticism and qualified the statement. 'In those distant days, to early peoples, they could well have seemed like giants.'

Duncan was unsure about the human origins his host was alluding to, assuming that it was apocryphal. Though if true the revelation could open up a remarkable Pandora's box. The academic in him still wasn't prepared for that. His authoritative knowledge could only be undermined so far.

Moses sensed the man's subconscious terror at being confronted by a challenge to his human identity. This archaeologist could accept that Homo sapiens and the Neanderthals interbred, and humans probably survived by becoming semi aquatic, living on the water's margins where there was a constant supply of food when the rest of the planet froze or became desert. Deeper than that, the lead boots of common sense would not take him.

Duncan Parfait had already been persuaded of enough and Moses did not want to drive his tame celebrity expert away by offering more than he could mentally digest in one sitting. So, while they waited for Miss Kandy, he offered him a coffee and aspirin instead.

Chapter 37

Kath and Neville sat in their car, doors wide open, silently contemplating the sea and hazy outline of France. Swifts vied in an aerial ballet, while pigeons flapped frantically to avoid the boisterous battles of crows and herring gulls.

The landscape on the South Coast had changed since Kath last knew it. Orchards that had been grubbed up were now being replanted and sea defences had grown higher. The popping of distant gunfire from an army range was still the same and the cliff they were parked near had been considerably eroded. The White Cliffs didn't seem as high as Kath remembered when watching Channel swimmers leave Dover, and the pervasive stench of decaying seaweed was no longer apparent in any of the places they had stopped at along the coast. Her world had unaccountably shrunk, apparently taking her sense of smell with it.

Neville had the uncanny knack of picking up on Kath's random thoughts when she least expected it. It was the last thing she had ever expected him to have in common with her ex-lover.

'Think if we sat here long enough we could become part of sea erosion?' he gently hinted.

'You want to move on?'

'Well, we did come all the way to meet this enigmatic paramour of yours. Seems a bit self-defeating to sit here watching a power station and container ships pass on the horizon.'

'You haven't an atom of romance in your soul, have you?'

'So let's go and meet the bloke who has. I might learn something.'

Kath gave in. She closed her door and turned the ignition. 'Don't blame me if he's not what you expect.'

'I've a feeling you're more worried that he won't be what you expect.'

The guest house they had booked rooms in was tucked away in a four-storey Victorian terrace and had a patio garden, small breakfast room, and never-ending stairs which Kath knew her encroaching arthritis was going to resent.

Kath and Neville's room was light, yet cosy. A herring gull mobile flapped in the sea breeze from an open window and its feathered counterparts outside screeched. It made Kath recall that the birds seldom slept and had persuaded Moses to have his bedroom windows triple glazed.

As they unpacked the suitcases she wondered whether she should have bought a small gift for Moses. It would have been received gratefully whatever it was and no doubt passed, regally, to the secretary/assistant she had not yet met. Probably not such a good idea, though she would definitely find something for Patsy who was still bound to be there.

'Stop working things out,' Neville chided. 'Everything will slot into place if you don't try too hard.'

'I like working things out. It's what women do. Pity men don't have the same gene.'

'All right,' he sighed. 'Let's pop into town and buy something for Patsy, then we can have a meal somewhere.'

'I hear there's a new upmarket restaurant in the harbour.'

'If it's that upmarket, it means we need to book. Fish and chips will suit me fine.'

Why not, Kath thought to herself, a good excuse for deep-fried calories, salt and vinegar.

Chapter 38

Maddie could tell that it meant trouble as soon as she opened the front door and saw the set of Lottie's jaw. She had often scalded Fred for keeping things to himself for fear of upsetting others. Keeping something that had been festering since childhood from his sister was liable to cause earth tremors.

'You need to see Fred?' Maddie enquired warily.

'Too bloody true,' announced Lottie.

'He's in the lounge painting papier mâché. Don't make him splatter paint on the carpet. I've just had it cleaned.'

'It's not paint you need to worry about.'

Fred and Maddie's large house was a celebration of the fact that they had been more productive in retirement than the so-called prime of life. It confirmed Lottie's suspicion that the only thing her brother had ever aspired to was collecting his pension.

Decorative bouquets, fairyland coats of arms, and dewy-eyed pets gazed out from cushions, hangings, and fire screens; all the result of Maddie's devotion to needlepoint. The glass fronted cabinets filled with flowers were also testament to her addiction to sugarcraft. Where the results of her expertise were not displayed, Fred's model ships, aeroplanes, and vintage cars were either suspended or arranged in dynamic tableau. Anyone entering the front door automatically tucked in their elbows for fear of knocking months of delicate work onto the stripped pine floor scattered with the rugs Maddie made before repetitive strain injury stopped her. Even the pergolas in the garden were flanked by industrious resin goblins from Fred's one and only attempt at modelling in that medium.

The practical and taciturn Lottie had always regarded her brother and his wife as human bower birds, forever displaying any object more ostentatious than the last.

Given her current state of mind, colliding with Fred's fragile models was the last thing that bothered her as she marched into the lounge where he was painting intricately curved eyebrows on a large octopus.

One glance over his half-moon spectacles told Fred that Lottie wasn't in the mood to admire his handicraft.

'Would it have been so bloody dreadful to mention that our father was a Nazi spy?' his sister blurted out to stop herself from exploding into a full-blown tantrum.

Fred had been practising how to deal with this inevitable moment for years.

He had been expecting it ever since she visited, Chapman, Chapman and Son. 'You doted on him,' he explained as conciliatorily as he dare.

'I barely remembered the man! You were just too spineless to tell me!'

'We couldn't let mother find out.'

'And you think I would have told her!?'

Fred's plan to defuse the situation started to unravel as his neck turned red with annoyed embarrassment.

'You've got a big mouth, Lottie. Always have had.'

Maddie could see that the worm that had been her husband was at last beginning to turn and felt reassured enough to leave and make coffee.

Lottie sat on the settee and faced her brother, his brush still defiantly poised to complete a delicate stroke.

'Octopuses don't have eyebrows Fred.'

'If you're under five, they do!' He put the brush down. 'Our father was a charismatic rat with opinions that would have terrified Pol Pot. The fact that he died in mysterious circumstances does not worry me in the slightest. It shouldn't worry you either.'

'He died in a bloody big explosion.'

Fred's jaw dropped. He knew his sister was a compulsive troublemaker, even if only for the good, but wasn't sure he wanted to know what she had dug up this time.

'What..?'

'There's a damn great crater where the centre of Fairdamon should be.'

'What the hell were you doing there? Nobody can get into that place.'

'Didn't it ever occur to you to go and look?'

Fred felt slightly abashed at the inference he was a wimp. 'Well no.'

'You obviously didn't believe our father was lost at sea, so why not?'

'As I said, the man was a traitor. I was just glad he

121

was dead and not liable to come back. Does it matter?'

Lottie hesitated. Now she had discovered the truth about her father, it shouldn't have really mattered. Fred was only being Fred in keeping the secret to himself after all. It was irrational to expect anything else of him.

'How can you be so sure he was there anyway?' asked Fred.

'Of course he was! Don't prevaricate!'

'That town's under quarantine, Lottie. The place could have been a death trap.'

'Bollocks. An anthrax bacterium doesn't survive that long. Those posters were just to keep out people who like to climb walls. It's never been used by the Army for manoeuvres. There's no way in for tanks.'

'How the hell did you get in then?'

'More to the point, what else are you keeping from me?'

Fred was affronted by the accusation. 'Nothing, I swear it. You know more than I do.' He took a deep breath. 'Look Lottie, You don't know what you're getting into. Please leave it alone.'

Maddie caught the last sentence as she brought in three mugs of coffee. 'Why should she, Fred? What possible interest could the authorities have in the place after all this time?'

Fred had dealt with enough "authorities" in his lifetime to know that they didn't let go that easily, but said nothing because he was outnumbered.

As Lottie felt her obsession with their treacherous father, Michael Freeman, wane, something else, intriguing, intangible, started to gnaw away at her. That she couldn't explain to her prosaic brother.

Chapter 39

What was his tame archaeologist going to make of this?

Moses almost wished the world described in the translation he had at last completed was less extraordinary. The librarian, Ko Tricali, who had been working on it three centuries ago evidentially came to the same conclusion and ensured that it never passed into the hands of an outsider. Here was the portrait of an ancient culture accomplished in technology and art in ways that were alien to later Fairdamons. Dr Duncan Parfait would have to suppress every last atom of his innate scepticism to read about a world where aircraft buoyed up by hot air sailed over the horizon like wandering clouds, mills were turned by geothermal energy, and olive green obsidian was ground into sheets to protect homes from the equatorial sun. Bright chemical dyes emblazoned buildings and clothes, and vehicles were drawn by compliant camel-like creatures now long extinct.

Moses still found the revelations astounding. His mother often told him tales which he assumed to be mythology. Now he had deciphered the ancient fragments for himself there could be no doubt that this was not fantasy, but a record of the way things used to be. He could remember having to fight back disbelief when she had told him that his people belonged to the stars, not the ragtag illusion anchoring others to reality's gutter. The pain of living may have seemed tangible to them, but the Fairdamon knew that it was a mere reflex at being briefly confined to mortality. Life was a wisp of evolution, a fine filament fastening it to a vast reality beyond the comprehension of any physical mind.

Moses also recalled his mother showing him how to close his eyes and think of nothing until light flooded his whole being. Only then would he realise that, when the last Fairdamon died, the link they had with reality would be severed, and everything they created on Earth dissolve back into the atoms it came from.

Since then he slowly began to understand the last request Allana Olandas asked of him. 'You are now the last guardian of Fairdamon. All its wealth is yours. Use it well and leave no evidence of us which will defame our memory. You are a child of the Cosmos, born of primeval forces.'

Despite an upbringing where the esoteric and mystical were taken as normal, Moses could never comprehend, let alone accept, that everything his people had ever achieved would eventually disappear when the last gene of its originators died. For all his precocious comprehension, he had been a realistic little boy. As he grew older, his mother was aware that her son would need to survive in a totally different world from the sheltered one she had known. So she told him no more tales about demons from another dimension and how everything Fairdamon, from the ruins of their cities to their artefacts, would dissolve at the passing of its last soul.

Moses Oradonte envied Duncan Parfait and Rolf Baker the prospect of reading the translation for the first time, and the chilling thrill they would experience when realising that this was not fantasy, but had been very real.

Before the translator could part with his years of work, though, the archaeologist had to be prepared. Moses did not expect this debunker of ancient conspiracy theories and magical civilisations to surrender his critical faculties overnight. It would also provide Moses with a last opportunity to marvel at what once had been, and then let go. If life is an illusion, as ancient Fairdamons believed, then would dreams endure beyond a mortal's passing? This last Fairdamon did not want to reach out to the dead, but embrace the all pervading light of a greater reality and swim in its warm, comforting sea... if only to escape that continual, gnawing pain...

He closed the binder filled with his meticulous handwriting and reached into the draw for the needle to deaden the reality which at that moment held him captive.

Chapter 40

The double garage contained one rarely used car and the rest of the space was crammed with all the oddments that wouldn't fit into the shed. Amongst them were discarded papier mâché experiments stacked up to the ceiling, the frame of a wheelless bicycle, no longer used workbench and boxes of Christmas tree decorations perched precariously on top of metal shelves, only stable because of the ancient sewing machine and toolbox anchoring the lowest shelf. Maddie had obviously attempted to organise the chaos, yet it had still managed to creep its way up to the door, leaving just enough space for the dustbin Fred was soaking papier mâché in and the piles of newspapers intended to feed it. Lottie had always wondered why her brother managed to make a life so laborious for himself when he could have much more easily carved his models from expanded polystyrene, not taking into account that would have left the house filled with a snow of white chippings.

Maddie had assumed Lottie to be the last person obsessed with recycling and sure enough it became apparent that as her sister-in-law rummaged furiously through the national broadsheets she was thinking about a brief snippet of news and not a paper mill.

'Not something possible to Google, then?'

'Tried it. Came up with dozens of irrelevant pages from the US, adverts for toxic slimming products, and half a dozen porno websites.'

'You should use a filter.'

'What, and miss diagnosing all those misaligned boobs and prolapses.'

'If Fred hadn't been making another papier mâché model for the children's centre all of these would have all been put in the recycling box you know.'

Lottie became so intent on scanning newsprint she barely heard. 'Big is it?'

'Huge. The octopus wasn't enough. Your brother now aspires to create a life-sized version of Botticelli's Venus rising from the sea...'

'Great.'

'Flanked by Daleks, cybermen, and Teletubbies.'

'Jolly good.'

'You're not listening to a word I say, are you?'

Lottie's stopped turning pages. 'Always knew Fred would go doolally, glueing all those matchsticks together when he was a boy.'

'What are you looking for, Lottie?'

'Article in the Telegraph, about three or four weeks ago. Read it in the Pastry Parlour over a coffee.'

Knowing Lottie, it could just as easily have been the Times or Observer. When it came to newspapers, they were all the same to someone who had no interest whatsoever in anyone else's political point of view.

Maddie pulled out several from a different pile. 'What was it about?'

'In the shorts. Man with supernatural sense of smell. Found some missing child when everyone else had given up.'

Maddie put her papers on the bonnet of the car near the open garage door. Her sister-in-law may have been able to see in the dimness of the garage light, but she needed her glasses to read anything smaller than a recipe book.

The speed with which Lottie continued to turn pages made Maddie wonder all the more what she was up to. This was the woman who had exposed the scam organised by a local hospital drug supplier and intimidated courtrooms when the prosecution called her in to testify as a special witness. Medical skills apart, Lottie would not accept the unexplained, inexplicable, or just downright unjust. No mystery she blundered into ever stood a chance. It was the way she went about dealing with them that worried Fred.

'What are you up to Lottie?' Maddie asked.

The doctor smiled at her in girlish surprise, which only confirmed Maddie's suspicions. 'Me? Up to?'

'I need to know if it's liable to give Fred a heart attack, or it just means the end of civilisation as we know it.'

'Nothing Maddie, I swear it. Believe me.'

'Of course I don't believe you. Just make sure you tell me before Fred finds out.'

'It's nothing that should worry him.'

'This isn't about your father, is it?'

But Lottie had gone back to scanning the news briefs.

While she was still deeply immersed in the Telegraph columns something in The Times caught Maddie's eye. Should she tell her sister-in-law or surreptitiously slip the newspaper into the bin where newsprint was dissolving for Fred's papier mâché? Unfortunately her sense of honesty was as acute as Lottie's sense of justice.

'Was the man's name Oradonte?'

The effect on Lottie was electric. She snatched the page from her. 'That's it! You're a star Maddie!'

Maddie could only wonder how many of Lottie's patients would have their treatment put on hold while the eccentric doctor yet again chased dragons. The knowledge that they could easily afford to pay for it stopped her feeling too much sympathy for them.

Chapter 41

Patsy was clipping bay trees in the front garden when Kath and Neville arrived.

The gardener immediately lowered the shears, intrigued to see how much Kath had changed over the years, and at last get a glimpse of the remarkable man who had stolen her away from the inscrutable Moses Oradonte. At least that was how she saw things through her purple-tinted view of the world. though both men would have undoubtedly disagreed. The Kath she remembered certainly would have; this had always been a woman with a mind of her own and would have resented any implication that she was a possession to be stolen by anyone.

Moses peered out from a front window, wondering why he had ever mentioned anything to Patsy. The woman had a good heart, but it had given her too much time to build up expectations which were bound to be dashed and that would bring out her judgemental side.

The regimented bay trees she resented so much would have been reduced to stumps if Kath and Neville hadn't appeared when they did. At least it had briefly taken Patsy away from lavishing attention on all the burgeoning flowers, bushes, and climbers producing so much pollen and perfume in the back garden.

As soon Neville came through the front gate Moses was initially taken aback by the man's balding homeliness, yet gratified to sense honesty in that comfortable charisma. It was also easy to tell that Patsy was fighting back her disappointment at Kath's portly partner as she dashed across the garden to greet them. Moses continued to watch with analytical detachment as Kath linked arms with Patsy to introduce her to Neville, registering every nuance of the trio as their insecure greetings contradicted the bold front they put on.

Wendy was also gazing down from her garret bedroom, wondering at the social interactions of a society she was sure she would never fully comprehend. She was unfamiliar with the couple and their complicated relationship with her employer. The English capacity to say everything but what they really meant could easily be detected from two storeys up. Should she remain in her spacious, airy apartment and pretend nothing was happening? The streptocarpuses were beginning to wilt and needed watering, and swifts nesting in the eaves were waiting for the dried insects she regularly sprinkled in the window box.

However much Wendy was entitled to her break, it was obvious that Moses wasn't going outside to greet them and give all the curtain twitchers in the vicinity something else to gossip about. Kath and Neville would have to be invited in, so she went downstairs. The neighbours had already built up a comprehensive fantasy about the wealthy recluse; his nocturnal vigils burning candles in the moss garden to commune with the dead, not to mention his secret drug habit. For all his expertise in reading other people, Moses had no idea how they found out about either. His garden was too well concealed to be overlooked, he was sure the rumours hadn't been spread by Wendy or Patsy and doubted that the Potion Professor gossiped about his clients. He could only hope that Kath didn't stay long enough to find out about his addiction. After persuading her to stop smoking, his morphine habit would have begged too many questions he didn't want to answer.

At least Neville turned out to be everything he had hoped; erudite, unassuming, totally honest, and still deeply in love with his partner.

Chapter 42

Dr Lottie Freeman was so expert at keeping her patients alive it wasn't often she had the need to visit a crematorium. In fact, the last occasion had been her mother's funeral.

The Vale was small compared to those sprawling, peaceful acres set aside for large residential areas and was relatively isolated, only needing to cater for the deceased of the small hamlets dotting that stretch of the coast.

It had taken some effort to track down the resting place of the last Oradonte and, given what Lottie had already found out, delving into the database of the Public Records Office must have rang at least one alarm bell. The doctor was sure as hell that it wasn't a coincidence that a dark hatchback now appeared to be following her. As the vehicle had clouded windows, it was not possible to tell what she was dealing with. So, just in case, Lottie took the monkey wrench from the back seat of the car where she had tossed it after her visit to Fairdamon and laid it on the passenger seat before driving up to the crematorium. Fortunately the hatchback stopped just outside the Vale. It didn't cross her mind that the driver might have known enough about her reputation to proceed very warily.

Lottie parked in a space reserved for visitors. Lime seeds crunched underfoot as she walked along the avenue up to the crematorium and baskets of fuchsias overhung commemorative plaques which were judiciously arranged around The Vale's boundary wall. There was no suggestion that the place concealed extraordinary secrets. Given that she only had a vague idea of what she was looking for, the doctor was not expecting to discover anything more surprising than an odd mutant gene

Lottie walked to the entrance where the sun's rays glinted on the brass of a freshly polished hearse and an elderly man dressed in an apron came out to greet her. By the way he was rolling down his sleeves he had been working on someone's dearly departed, making them presentable before being committed to the flames.

Lottie's enquiry about a client from over two decades ago was met with enthusiasm, and not the discreet reluctance usually encountered; the fact that it had been made by a doctor possibly helped. She was shown into a small office adjoining the main funeral parlour and chapel. There was an open box of makeup on the desk which the mortician tactfully closed and placed on a shelf before taking down an old register of deaths.

As soon as Lottie mentioned the name Oradonte, he lifted a knowing finger. 'Of course, I remember the family well. No funeral services. First the father - I didn't cremate him; that was done by the first owner - then the Oradonte's son - really tragic that. Then lastly the mother. Wonderful looking woman. None of the deceased came from a church. Well remember our local cleric announcing that they were all Gnostics and didn't deserve the name of Jesus to be mentioned over their heretical bodies. The way they had managed to keep themselves to themselves in this gossipy neighbourhood really annoyed him. And us around here always suspected our vicar was a child molester anyway.'

Lottie had no wish to get involved in another campaign, especially over a long dead paedophile man of God so, while the mortician turned the pages of the register, she wandered out into the small chapel filled with white lilies. The air was still and heavy with the heavy scent of Lilium regale and, without warning, the sensation of her own mortality which she had experienced in Fairdamon overwhelmed her.

Lottie shuddered. Even though death held no terrors for her - she was well aware how humdrum and mundane it could be - there was something else niggling away at her. It was as though the Oradontes had left their secret lingering in the silence with all the other souls that had passed over.

Lottie dismissed the intrusive thought. There were many things she intended to do before joining her deceased patients who were liable to demand why their treatment hadn't worked. The mystery of life and the Universe would be an open book to her all in good time. Then and there, there was another conundrum needed solving and.

She returned to the elderly mortician who had just

131

discovered the last Oradonte entry in the register.

'This mother, what was so remarkable about her?'

'Her hair,' he explained. 'She had the goldest of hair, and it wasn't out of a bottle.'

Lottie detected guilt in his tone. 'You snipped a few strands as a memento, didn't you?'

He shrugged; he was too old to care about being reprimanded for unprofessional conduct, and well aware Lottie had a different agenda so was unlikely to be bothered about the morality of it. 'There are those who will "liberate" the odd gold ring when there are no relatives to hand it on to, but I was never tempted. Not until I saw that woman. Wonderful she was. Never seen another human like her. Death usually removes the aura of what a person used to be, but I felt I could still speak to her and she would hear, maybe not in this existence, but from somewhere.'

'You didn't take enough hair to part with a few strands, did you?'

The mortician wasn't surprised; doctors often had pet projects of their own that involved collecting samples of the deceased. 'For DNA analysis?'

Lottie took a quick breath and cursed herself for sounding too obvious. 'There is a line of research in which it might prove useful.'

At last mortician's and doctor's gazes met as they realised that they were sharing the same, hugely unlikely, suspicion.

'We should both be past having fantastical ideas like that,' he observed.

'Perhaps we are both old enough to know that fact can be stranger than fiction.'

'If you do find out what we suspect, please don't tell me. I wouldn't have the stamina to persuade whoever's in that car which followed you here that I know nothing.'

'Then perhaps you had better let me have all the hair, just in case you are persuaded to hand it over.'

If they were right, Lottie had no intention of telling

the mortician anyway. He was too honest to carry the secret of something so unsettling to his deathbed.

'I'll get it.' The old man bustled to an alcove filled with drawers.

Lottie pulled on some examination gloves and took out a sterile phial, wondering if the same suspicions had crossed the treacherous mind of her father. Thankfully it was unlikely. What the Third Reich would have done with that knowledge didn't bear thinking about.

Chapter 43

Kath had anticipated that Moses would have become more eccentric and introverted in his self-imposed isolation. Her apprehension was unfounded. If anything, he had blossomed in his confined, luxurious world, no doubt helped by taking midnight strolls to avoid holidaymakers and dog walkers, and returning to spend the early hours sitting in the sanctuary of his moss garden to contemplate the world by candlelight.

Of course, Moses was careful that Kath didn't find out that this contentment had more to do with morphine than inner peace. She had no idea of the effort it took to walk with her to the viewing platform where they looked out over a silver sea stretching away into a haze that concealed France and the container ships plying its coast.

The air was unusually still for such a coastal high point and Kath became aware of the difficulty he had in breathing. 'That sounds like asthma?'

Moses tried to shrug it off, yet was grateful for any excuse to sit down. 'Only a touch.'

They went to a seat from where they could watch noisy children and wayward dogs from a safe distance, though one Staffie did wander over to Moses and fix him with an enquiring gaze until its owner called it back.

'I thought dogs are meant to be kept on leads?' said Kath.

'So should their owners.' He paused to watch a herring gull swoop down on a discarded chip. It flapped, cackling loudly, back into the sky after leaving a dropping which caught the sunlight to sparkle jewel-like in the newly mown grass.

Then Moses closed his eyes and drank in the stillness, for once not even disturbed by the screeching gulls. Kath allowed him to silently muse as she had always done, not knowing where his meandering thoughts were taking him.

These irrational excursions into his subconscious were increasing, as though he was being prepared for a greater adventure. They made little sense as he was drawn into an ancient world he still had difficulty in believing could have been real. Surely no clouds on Earth were ever that colour.

Unable to resist the candyfloss dimension, his thoughts floated away. Moses found himself wandering along a footpath leading to a city which clung to a huge craggy outcrop. It was suspended like an elegant carbuncle on the nose of the mountain's god as though sneezed out with all the precious minerals harboured in its breast. Airships came and went like hoverflies, small wings beating vigorously as they docked on platforms overhanging an abyss to unload their cargoes. A golden carriage carrying dignitaries rose into the peach coloured clouds like a bird gleaming with its own importance.

All seemed well with this world.

Then Moses felt a rumble deep in the earth. A fissure appeared in the cliff face above the overhang. He watched, awestruck, as the city slowly fell away from the mountain in a glittering cascade of glass, alabaster, limestone and brightly clad bodies.

Kath noticed Moses suddenly twitch and knew it would have been like waking a sleepwalker to disturb him.

He didn't fall with the fabulous ruins. Instead his reverie carried him far away to a valley where long extinct ungulates wandered about, browsing and glancing in his direction to ensure he was no threat. A rodent the size of a small car plodded by to paddle in a lake's margin and camels with necks the length of a giraffe's appeared down haughtily. Then a giraffe with large horns and neck no longer than a stag's emerged from the camouflage of trees with huge angular leaves.

His thoughts had never taken Moses back so far in time before. It felt peaceful here, with not even a similon to sink its teeth into the browsers. Perhaps it was all part of a journey that he knew would soon come to an end. Believing that, he was able to relax and let the dream slip away. Kath would not ask where he had been - she had never done so before.

Moses opened his eyes.

'You haven't changed,' she said.

'Of course I have.'

'You're still a recluse, just as wealthy, and with nowhere to go. I at least expected you to have another girlfriend by now... Not unless it's Wendy?'

'She has far too much sense, and a large family in the Philippines to support on the pittance I pay her.'

Kath smiled. Whatever foibles Moses had, stinginess was not one of them.

'So why did you want to see me? Why now, after being so adamant we should never meet again?'

'Can I not change my mind about just one thing?'

'Yes, as long as I know the reason why.'

'I now spend too much time wandering in my thoughts instead of being gainfully employed.'

'Does that mean you have finished translating that stack of gobbledygook at long last?'

Moses tried not to flinch at her attempt to annoy; Kath was well aware how much his secret endeavour meant to him. 'There is little more I can add.'

'And what happens to it now?'

Moses gave a secretive smile. 'I have found just the

135

person who will appreciate its tortuous saga.'

'Can I read it?'

'No. You are not old enough.'

'You mean that I never took it seriously. Just one chapter?'

'History does not have chapters. Apart from that, you could never finish any book without sex on every other page and plenty of murders.'

'You forgot about the volcanic eruptions and alien invasions.'

'I will bequeath to you that complete set of Doctor Who you left behind instead. They must be collectable by now.'

'You only bought them to please me. Now I have all of them on DVD, and you'll never watch any episodes before you die. '

Hardly where the words out of Kath's mouth when she was stabbed by the icy laser of awareness. Moses was gazing out to sea and didn't notice the change in her expression even if he detected her small gasp.

'I also purchased Babylon 5,' he went on benignly.

I know. But they were on video as well. The tapes must have deteriorated by now.'

'Wendy watched most episodes. I had to persuade her not to take them to a charity shop where all yesterday's best productions seem to end up.'

'Got the most stylish clothes in my wardrobe from them.'

Moses understood why Kath would not ask why she had been invited to see him again. 'I am sorry.'

'Sorry?'

'Truly sorry. However, as that old cliché goes, some things can never be.'

Kath had never really understood why it was impossible for Moses to give her children, even back then there had been so many advances in IVF, and no man could have had sperm that reluctant. There was little point in bringing it up again... Especially now.

Chapter 44

Lottie had only ever possessed one copy of Gray's Anatomy, and she had no idea where it went too. Volumes twice that size could easily get lost in her consulting room's overloaded shelves crammed with encyclopaedias, books on anthropology, chemistry, quantum theory and biology. There were surprisingly few tomes on medicine and she had no idea how the Catherine Cookson first edition from a grateful patient had somehow managed to sneak its way onto a shelf. Why Mrs Maddison thought that her physician would have been interested in the sexual lives of older women was a mystery, though it was more likely her intention to suggest that Dr Freeman get one. The patient had no way of knowing that Lottie's only foray into a relationship had ended in disaster and cured her of wanting another one. Why jump into the murky pond of human emotions when you could fish patients from it and turn a profit prescribing tranquillisers? And every so often a genuinely interesting condition would turn up and give her the satisfaction of diagnosing an ailment that had baffled specialists.

Mr Gibson Hunter was one of Lottie's trickier patients who had been obliged to go private when NHS GPs were no longer willing to cope with his foibles. This nonagenarian didn't care how much it cost; he just wanted a doctor to reassure him that he could carry on misbehaving like a 13-year-old without any ill effects. If he hadn't been prepared to pay enough to cover her surgery's ground rent, she would have just passed him on to another doctor to have his cantankerousness dismissed as signs of dementia. Having put up with the problem patient for the last 20 years without him flinching at her acerbic diagnoses, Lottie saw no point in bouncing him now.

'Kippers and jam should not be eaten together. One before the other, preferably with bread, would help you digests them.'

'I'm gluten intolerant!' snapped the old man.

'No you are not. You never have been.'

'I want a second opinion.'

'All right.' Lottie looked directly into eyes that shouldn't have sparkled so much given their age, and repeated, 'You are not gluten intolerant.'

Mr Gibson Hunter may have been used to this overworked ploy, but wasn't one to give up that easily. 'What about irritable bowel syndrome?'

'You have indigestion,' his doctor insisted patiently. 'If you were to eat ready prepared meals from Waitrose instead of spending so much time in McDonald's, your stomach wouldn't give you any problems.'

'I like looking at the scantily clad girls in there.'

'There is nothing I can prescribe for being a dirty old man.'

'You should see the size of some of them. Skimpy tops and tights with enough fat hanging out for any fit man to get a grip on.'

'Don't count on being too old to be locked up for sexual harassment.'

'Me? I could never get hold of one with my carpal tunnel.'

Thankfully Lottie's phone rang. Normally she would have allowed it to be picked up by the answerphone, but any excuse was welcome to cut short a consultation with Mr Gibson Hunter.

She lifted the receiver despite the furrowed disapproval of the patient who expected her undivided attention. 'Yes, this is Dr Freeman... oh, hello... I didn't expect the results so quickly.' She listened as the geneticist confirmed the extraordinary conclusion Lottie had already come to before putting the hair sample in the post. 'I see... No, it had been kept in reasonably sterile conditions. The only likely contamination would have been human...'

Even the self-obsessed Mr Gibson Hunter registered the change in his usually cool and collected doctor. Enough blood had left her features to reveal the mesh of broken veins on her cheeks and port wine stains he had always assumed to be large freckles. He also suddenly became aware that the Lottie he had always regarded as a much younger woman was well into her 70s.

As she continued to listen to the geneticist on the other end of the phone resolve hardened her expression and a flush at having discovered something momentous returned the colour to her cheeks.

Lottie became aware that her patient taking everything in. The man may have been a delinquent, but he wasn't senile and filled his waking hours, which was most of them, with gossip as well as eating all the wrong things.

She told the geneticist, 'No, I would much prefer that this was kept between us, not unless you want to risk having your lab's competence assessed or being ridiculed in the Lancet... I know... This will just have to remain one of Nature's mysteries. Why not fax me the results - Don't e-mail them! - And destroy the evidence... Yes, the hair sample as well.'

Lottie slowly lowered the receiver, well aware that Mr Gibson Hunter's imagination was working overtime. Fortunately his scientific knowledge was pre Niels Bohr, when it had been assumed the sun was a huge lump of coal blazing in the sky. What she had just learnt was so extraordinary, and went against any scientific knowledge he possessed, the old man had no way of guessing what the phone call had really been about. At the worst, he would spread a rumour that she had snatched samples from an alien autopsy.

As his physician had spent so much time talking to someone else, this patient thought he at least had the right to know who had interrupted the consultation. 'Who was that?'

Lottie leaned back and fixed the old man with a disconcerting gaze. 'Have you ever thought about mortality, Mr Gibson Hunter?'

'God no. Mostly sex. It's what keeps me going.'

Lottie didn't doubt that for one moment, and wrote out a prescription for indigestion powder.

Chapter 45

After his mounting curiosity to meet his partner's ex-lover, Neville was not disappointed. The man was just as enigmatic, and self-contained as he had expected. Unlike Kath's, his preconceptions ended there and Neville knew that Moses Oradonte was seriously ill as soon as he spoke.

'How long do you intend to stay?'

'We booked for three days, though it depends on what the local shopping is like,' Neville admitted.

'Yes, Kath always had an addiction for second-hand outlets.'

Neville smiled at his hardly disguised disapproval. 'Furnished our house from them, she did. Hallelujah for other people rejects.' He was unable to resist stroking the green velvet of his moss seat. 'This is amazing. Think Kath would like a moss garden?'

'Her tastes are like Patsy's. She prefers plants to fluoresce like storm beacons and throw out enough perfume to stun the sparrows.'

It had been a pointless question. Neville knew quite well that his partner veered towards the livid end of the spectrum when it came to decorating: he had spent half a lifetime trying to accommodate her tastes, leaving one small workroom in muted colours for himself where he could allow his retinas to relax. It now seemed all the more extraordinary that Kath and Moses had ever got together.

'Kath can be a bit strange as well.' Neville was barely aware that he had said it aloud.

Moses mischievously picked up on his faux pas. 'As well as whom?'

There was no point in blustering with embarrassment now the words were out. 'As you.'

Far from being offended, Moses gave a contented smile. Yes, this was the very man he needed. Duncan Parfait was self-promoting, passionate, and verging on self-tortured dipsomania, yet both men had an honest integrity he was lucky to find twice in the same year.

It was time to let Neville know why he was there. 'I have a terminal illness.'

Neville said nothing; he had already guessed as much.

'And need an executor.'

That did take him aback. The thought of handling the affairs of Kath's wealthy ex-lover hadn't entered his head, though it was the perfect explanation for why he had been invited to visit him.

'Me?'

'The young Miss Kandy is an efficient solicitor, but ambitious and could move on to better prospects at any time, leaving my affairs in the hands of someone less able.'

'Is this where I ask how much you're worth?'

'Must be many millions. If you are willing to accept my request, I shall introduce you to my accountant. I have no doubt he can produce a more accurate figure.'

Apart from being surprised, Neville was flattered to encounter someone who believed that his only skills weren't limited to making toys which would be destroyed by grandchildren and teaching young people how to grow houseplants. For all his practical achievements, the trust this mysterious, wealthy man was prepared to invest in him gave his ageing ego a rejuvenating boost.

'I will, of course, ensure that you are reasonably compensated,' Moses added, gratified that it hadn't yet crossed his guest's mind.

Neville recoiled at the suggestion. 'God no! Kath would demand to know where the money came from. She'd never forgive me for not consulting her first.' He hesitated. 'Does she know how ill you are?'

'She has guessed, though it was not my intention to

tell her.'

'I won't mention it until...'

Moses nodded. 'No funeral. I insist on that.'

'Why not?'

'It would be wasted on a nonbeliever and only attended by Patsy, Wendy and the neighbourhood drug dealer.'

'Lack of a funeral will also be difficult to explain.'

Moses never said that was Neville's problem, though it was obvious he would have to work out how to handle it when the time came.

There was a more immediate formality to deal with. 'I am afraid we will need to visit my solicitor to get the papers signed.'

'Doesn't she do house calls?'

'I am apparently worth so much, and undertaking like this away from her office would make Miss Kandy nervous. This way, she can be totally sure that I am not under any duress.'

Neville chuckled. 'Can't believe that you could be bullied into anything. It's not as if you're giving me the power of attorney.' He looked up quickly. 'You're not, are you?'

'I would not dream of it. I intend to die with my mental faculties intact, even if nothing else about me is.'

'You have more bottle than I have. Me, I'd go out in a drunken stupor.'

'There will be morphine of course.'

'Shouldn't there be a doctor, though?' Something profoundly unsettling occurred to Neville. 'You're not being treated for this condition, are you?'

'There would be no point.'

'Why not?'

'All my family died of it. There is no cure.'

'You sound very certain of that?'

Moses realised that the suspicions of the easy-going Neville had been aroused. 'My ancestry is somewhat unusual. The condition is very rare and I do not wish it

142

to attract any physician who would like to use it for research. When I die, the illness dies with me.'

Neville respected Moses' defensiveness and decided not to press the point. He certainly wouldn't have wanted to become the subject of medical research, so could empathise with his antipathy towards doctors. There was one concern, though. 'If you are determined to go out on morphine, better to have a doctor there to make sure it's the right dose.'

'I would not dream of asking one to take that risk.'

'What about Wendy?'

'She will be spending a few days with her family in the Philippines.'

No, Neville thought, he hadn't underestimated the man.

Chapter 46

When Liz opened the door to Meg's council flat, and was confronted by a professional woman with unsmiling, angular features she assumed her to be from social services. Believing that she had at last been caught out for claiming rent fraudulently, the young mother's first instinct was to slam the door and abseil from the balcony with the baby she clutched; her second to lock herself in the bathroom. Liz's indecision, and the fact she wasn't quite sober, allowed Lottie Freeman to enter before any sensible reflex could prevent it.

'Elizabeth Dawson?'

The tone of authority demanded a reply.

'Yeah... Who are you?'

'A doctor.'

Liz would have dropped baby Donnie with relief if Lottie hadn't caught him.

'You here to see her then?'

'No, it's not a medical matter.'

Liz's addled alarm once again rose. 'What then?'

'I simply have a physician's interest in the way your daughter was discovered by someone with such an acute sense of smell.'

'Oh yeah...' Scientific research was not something Liz thought about that much.

'It's purely medical curiosity. Nothing more.'

Reassured as well as flattered that someone had at last taken a genuine interest in her petulant, screechy Angie, Liz invited the visitor into the kitchen where she made them a mug of tea each. Lottie sat at the table, still clutching baby Donnie who gazed at her in amazed curiosity while his mother prattled on.

'Silly little cow's got to stop doing that sort of thing. Police really got upset that time.'

'I could imagine,' agreed Lottie. 'She seems to have been a very lucky little girl.'

'Gord knows how he did it. They even had a dog trying to pick up her scent from a cardigan - I knew I shouldn't have used that cheap fabric softener. It made it all fluffy and smell like a brothel.'

Now a tracker dog had entered the equation, this helped to confirm the extraordinary DNA results. No human the doctor had ever encountered, medically or otherwise, possessed olfactory senses as acute as a canine's.

'Lucky mum knows Patsy,' Liz went on, 'If she hadn't asked him, he would never have come. He's a strange guy, keeps himself to himself. Lives up on the cliff in one of those big houses near the church. Apparently got Patsy to make this moss garden for him and had her lay out his front garden like one of those fancy ornamental ones they had in palaces - like chequerboard.'

Thank you very much, Lottie thought to herself; it was just what she needed to know. 'I understand he's not too well?'

'Got this horrible cough. Had to leave the party we held for him early.' Liz lowered her voice. 'They say he takes drugs, and rumour says his family had inbreeding problems. You're a doctor - you must know all about that sort of thing.' She stopped in mid-flow as a something occurred to her. 'What did you say your name was, by the way?'

For a moment, Lottie thought she had got away with that. 'Dr Freeman, Dr Lottie Freeman.'

'Oh...' said Liz, and promptly forgot it as she prattled on, telling her visitor everything it would have taken far more effort to obtain from a reasonably sensible person.

Meg had been quietly smoking a cigarette on the balcony and didn't realise Liz had a visitor until she heard them chatting through the open kitchen window. By the time she realised what was going on it was too late to dash in and tell Liz to shut up. All she could do was take out her mobile phone.

'Hello Patsy?.. Yeah, me... Something you should know...'

Chapter 47

The mobile home that Moses Oradonte had given Patsy sat in its own large plot which produced most of the vegetables, herbs and fruit for the house. Wendy, who insisted on cooking for everyone, initially had problems with British ingredients, though adapted and was soon preparing everything from mushroom risottos to broad bean salads. The health of Patsy's husband, Andy, improved on the diet and he was soon able to spend most of the time weeding, watering and pruning as far as his last stroke would allow.
Kath wondered how the gardener had time to keep her home so tidy, especially as it was filled with Romany knickknacks and more varieties of flowers than she stocked in her florist shop.

After a mint infusion with honey, Patsy invited her outside.

The two women were aware that Moses was

watching them as they wandered about the large garden that he seldom ventured into. Little had changed since Kath last saw it, even the rampant lilies of the valley were still determined to colonise the fruit trees. Within its high walls, Patsy had indulged her fancy; from a secret garden to a Mediterranean corner filled with exotics more used to a desert climate. Neville had already been taken on the tour and had been astounded at the gardener's achievement. Even the compost bins were covered in morning glory while opportunistic nasturtiums defiantly burst out like flames from the breaks on the paths that campanula hadn't already colonised.

Patsy picked a ripe apricot from a branch and handed it to Kath. 'These shouldn't be ready so early. Come to that, they shouldn't be growing here at all,' she observed proudly, and then qualified it, 'This is a sun trap and we have our own water supply. Tank below stores rainwater and it's piped round the garden.'

Suddenly Kath felt herself craving warmer climates. With an irrigation system like that she could have grown her own pot plants in the garden and cut out Neville, the middleman. Then, perhaps not. Grubbing around in the soil wasn't her style and the only twine she wanted to tie was around bouquets.

Kath took a bite of the apricot, expecting it to be sharp; instead it was pleasantly sweet. 'What happens to this fruit? You, Wendy, and Moses can hardly eat it all?'

'I take it to the farmers' market and donate the proceeds to charity.'

Ever the businesswoman, Kath wondered what the other stallholders thought about that, and then was surprised to realise that she really didn't care. In Patsy's privileged position, she would have done exactly the same thing.

As they passed a small greenhouse, pots of bright colours caught her attention. 'Who are the streptocarpus for?'

'Wendy. She isn't obsessed with much, but has to buy each new hybrid as soon as Dibley's produce it. Can't keep them downstairs because of you-know-who, and her bedroom's running out of space.' Patsy opened the door. 'Like a few from the lents I've divided? Save lugging them to the market.'

'Sure Wendy won't mind?'

'She'll be glad enough if they go to a good home.'

'Thanks a lot. I promise not to put them in the shop.'

'You think they look good enough to sell in your florists?'

'Of course they do, Patsy. You're the best. Always have been. You're wasted on a man disabled by his olfactory senses and who only wants to be surrounded by moss.'

'Tell me about it. The money's very good, though. Most other gardeners my age have retired.'

Kath discreetly turned her back to the house, unsure whether Moses could lip read from that distance. 'Just how ill is he?'

Patsy knew that it was pointless to prevaricate, so opened the greenhouse door and beckoned her to follow. 'Wendy could tell you, though never mentions it. I've seen him in pretty bad shape, and I know she gets his supply of morphine somehow.'

It shouldn't have come as a shock, but Kath still had trouble accepting how ill Moses was. 'Oh god...'

'Sorry.'

'All his family went the same way. I should be surprised that he lasted this long.'

'You knew his mother, didn't you?'

'Briefly. Extraordinary woman. Used to talk for hours without giving anything away, and boy, did that family have secrets. And I don't mean skeletons in the cupboard.'

'Are there are any other sort?'

'I think it had more to do with what they could see

147

through the cracks of reality.'

'I know what you mean, but it's all too deep for me.' The gardener put several pots of streptocarpus in a trug. 'I look at it this way, there's no point in trying to work out the meaning of Life, the Universe, and Everything, because you're sure as hell going to find out what it's all about eventually anyway.'

Kath nodded; she had always believed the Oradontes understood that before passing into the mysterious quantum absurdity of death - or whatever else it turned out to be. That was why she would never confront Moses about his condition. He was bound to be dealing with it in his own mysterious way, so it was best to leave well alone. The real tragedy probably was his allergy to pollen, which prevented him from appreciating the beauty of a flower like an African primrose with their pastel trumpets dappled like exotic moths.

Chapter 48

Duncan held his breath as the bank manager left and sealed the outer door of the vault after him.

The chamber that was revealed coruscated in the hard fluorescent light like a crystal encrusted geode. The archaeologist wouldn't have dared step inside without the urging of Moses: something throwing out so much brilliance had to be radioactive.

So Duncan took a deep breath. He had been at the opening of ancient tombs and handled ornaments not touched for millennia, yet, for the first time in his career, he was daunted. Unique pieces this ancient should not have gleamed so much unless they had been lovingly tended from the mists of time.

He plucked up the courage to touch an artefact, and then gently lift it... and then another, and another, he is fingers tingling with excitement.

Many of the ceramics amongst the carved rock

crystal and gleaming gold were in immaculate condition while others had inevitably been chipped, corroded, or crazed with age. Infuriatingly, Duncan couldn't identify one of them. For all his expertise the contents of the Oradontes' secret vault might just as well have arrived from outer space. Even the winged effigies bore no resemblance to the jinn or mystical deities excavated in the Orient. Some even had the heads of animals he knew to be extinct, while others depicted people who, to his certain knowledge, did not appear in any of the most ancient of papyri or wall paintings he was familiar with.

Moses had anticipated that his guest would be struck dumb with wonder and said nothing to break his astounded silence. He had no intention of manipulating the archaeologist, just waited patiently until he was prepared to admit that the artefacts were genuine. Duncan was experienced enough to know a hoax, however carefully planned, and would not have been taken in by Piltdown man for a second. Having already established that the statuette Moses sent him preceded human civilisation as he knew it, he was convinced that these creations were just as ancient. Everything in the vault seemed to come from the same culture and could have even predated the Toba eruption 72,000 years ago.

As Duncan examined each amber carving, ornament of precious metal and obsidian tool, he could only imagine what the makers of these remarkable items would have been able to craft with glass.

Moses observed, 'There were many pieces too fragile to move. The glass would have disintegrated at the touch.'

Duncan was so absorbed as he continued to examine some vessels carved from alabaster, carnelian and jade, he didn't wonder how Moses had read his mind. Examination with a magnifying glass did not reveal any marks to identify their creators: they evidently didn't crave recognition. There was a much lighter, freer - even humorous - feel to these artefacts than those from the later civilisations he was familiar with. They reflected a world of relaxed luminosity far from the squalid hand to mouth existence of the hunter gatherer. Their lives must have been blessed by a stable and benign climate to allow such a pitch of sophistication. But when? There was no precedent with which to date the remarkable hoard.

'How old?' Duncan eventually asked.

Moses shrugged apologetically. 'I have no idea.'

The archaeologist should have realised it was an impossible question. Items of such antiquity would hardly have brought a provenance with them. Their authentication and dating could only be calculated by scientists and an open mind. It was a salutary to know that Moses had not shown this treasure of such untold value to anyone else. Duncan hoped he could keep his nerve long enough to make the right decision about what to do. He would never be able to walk from the vault into daylight without an image of the glorious artefacts imprinted into the back of his mind. More to the point, what was Moses expecting him to do with the knowledge? One man alone, even Dr Duncan Parfait, surely wasn't expected to undermine the fixed preconceptions of his profession, however much turning Devil's advocate now appealed to him?

The archaeologist was allowed to linger in the Aladdin's cave of prehistoric treasure until the bank manager discreetly returned to ensure there was still enough oxygen in the vault to support life.

Only after being assured that he would soon have all the time in the world to examine them in a purpose-built museum, did the archaeologist reluctantly agree to leave.

As the bank's outer door silently slid aside, fresh air and traffic fumes hit Duncan with reality's mallet and his knees almost buckled. He was overwhelmed by the realisation that there were not only hundreds of undersea sites to be excavated, but the Oradonte's huge collection to be catalogued, drawn, and photographed for disbelievers and posterity, not to mention the obligatory carbon dating tests.

Duncan's wildest aspirations now made reality, he was Alice in Wonderland where the doctrines he had been committed to all his life no longer applied.

The archaeologist needed a stiff drink and someone acquiescent to rant at.

Chapter 49

By the time the Rolf joined Duncan in the Rat and Compass, his mentor was barely able to stand without the aid of the counter. It was obvious something else even more profound than ancient maps had shaken his normally unflappable colleague. Rolf manoeuvred him into a corner nook and ordered coffee in the hope it would sober him up enough to discover what it was. Despite shaking hands with antediluvian fairies at that moment, Duncan was aware of the irony that his junior partner would turn out to be the more mature in the face of momentous discovery.

'Did our remarkable ancients have a use for alcohol, do you think?' Rolf asked as he returned with two inky coffees strong enough to descale a kettle.

Duncan shook his tangled hair. 'They could fly without it...'

Rolf hesitated, unsure whether this should be taken as a statement of fact or something the green fairy was whispering in his ear. He suspiciously eyed the dregs of viridian in Duncan's glass. 'What have you been drinking for pity's sake?'

'A cocktail.'

Rolf groaned. If it was one mixed by Flo from her secret stash in the cellar it probably contained absinthe. The woman would have lost her licence years ago if it weren't for her invention of another beverage, which was known locally as the stomach pump. Rolf

151

would have ordered one for Duncan if he had not been so impatient to find out the reason for his inebriated perplexity.

'Think you can keep down a chip butty?' he asked warily.

Duncan spread his arms like a lead doorstop with aspirations of flight.

Rolf caught the table lamp before it hit the floor.

'I could keep down half a dozen of the best pugilists this pub can offer.'

'Just try to keeping your voice down instead. This is not a good place to make that sort of declaration.' Rolf pushed a coffee towards him. 'Get this down you.'

Duncan gave his researcher a studied look as though seeing him for the first time. 'My little boy is growing up.'

'If you don't sober up, I'm phoning Carol to come and fetch you.'

Without further argument, Duncan downed both mugs of the brew known by the regulars as rat crap and, when he could at last focus again, realised what an idiot he was making of himself.

'How did I do?' he asked shamefacedly.

'Well, I always said this place should have a cabaret.' Rolf smiled ruefully at Flo who was merrily polishing evidence of other toxic misdemeanours from glasses. 'God, this dive should be closed down. At least it must be the only pub in London where the locals are seldom sober enough to recognise who you are.'

Two chip butties dripping with brown sauce were thrust onto the table before them by the small, effervescent Millie.

'Bon appetite,' she wished them optimistically before bustling back into the smoke-filled kitchen.

'Now,' said Rolf, 'what have you found?'

Duncan's head fell back onto the antimacassar of his faded tapestry chair and he stared at the ceiling still discoloured by a century of smokers. 'Wonderful things... Wonderful things...'

Chapter 50

As they drove away Kath turned to take one last look back at Moses Oradonte, knowing it would be the last time they met. She was now convinced that he was terminally ill but, like so many other secrets, Moses had kept that to himself as well. It was almost overwhelming for her to think about his impending death.

Neville was aware what she was thinking and said nothing. He could accept being his partner's second choice after such a remarkable man, and even be thankful he met Moses Oradonte. The man's other-worldliness had cast an inexplicable allure impossible for his practical mind to fathom.

The couple remained silent as they drove over the downs and through lush green valleys until a landscape of fields and woodland opened up before them. Arcades of trees led to prettily planted villages with mediaeval histories. They had survived revolution, plague and starvation when other less fortunate hamlets were now just stains under ploughed fields, which had endured because of prosperous newcomers intent on living like Tudor lords and more realistic, albeit judicious, redevelopment to allow in the 20th century - if not the 21st.

Kath experienced an odd longing for places she had never lived in, only passed through, while Neville fought back the suspicion that, despite his assurances, Moses had bequeathed them more than enough to buy one of those desirable properties with Elizabethan barns or converted oast houses.

He could stand it no longer. 'Odd fellow, Moses.'

'Always has been,' Kath agreed. 'The oddest thing is, I could never quite work out why.'

'How do you mean?'

'He wasn't really that peculiar when I think about it. Asthma can make a recluse of some people. There was just something about him...'

Neville nodded. There was nothing in the man's conversation that had suggested he was any more eccentric than many others, yet there was still something unfathomable about the man. Not having a huge imagination, Neville would have been astounded if he ever found out what it was. It was just as well, as his executor, that he was happily oblivious of what the Oradontes' bank vault contained.

Chapter 51

It was no good; the shadow that had attached itself to Lottie after the visit to Fairdamon was still following her. However many detours, twists and turns she took to shake it off, the car continued to dog her progress like an annoying black beetle trapped in her slipstream. Before, it hardly mattered; now she needed to pay a house call where secrecy was imperative.

Putting her DOCTOR ON CALL notice in the windscreen, Lottie parked in a lay-by near a mobile cafe selling snacks to lorry drivers. There were a few puzzled glances as customers wondered which one of their number had been found slumped over the wheel. When the doctor got out of her car and slammed its door with unnecessary force, they weren't inclined to ask.

The black car tailing her had no choice but to drive on and pull up on the verge further ahead to avoid leaving the slip road and losing its quarry.

Burly lorry drivers stepped aside as the septuagenarian physician marched through their masticating number and watched in overt fascination as she strode to the black car parked up ahead beyond two lorries and a pantechnicon.

The screaming of swifts circling above heightened the tension as Lottie hammered the car's side window.

His view obscured by the lorries, the driver hadn't been expecting the short, furious woman to confront her pursuer. Usually an agent with nerves of steel, he jumped and, when the doctor indicated with her thumb that he get out of the car for a brief consultation, he automatically obeyed. Any other person would have been intimidated by the tall young man towering above them. Not Lottie. Intimidation had been attempted by the best and never worked yet. For someone who spent a considerable amount of time behind the wheel of a car, the agent's raincoat was pointlessly long, almost ankle length, and looked like a bespoke heirloom from the mid-20th-century. Beneath it his summer suit was modern, expensive and casual, somewhat at odds with the taut expression that suggested he was not quite cut out for a life of espionage. Highly qualified in some subject totally irrelevant to his vocation, he was nevertheless determined to make the best of it. It was his misfortune to encounter Dr Lottie Freeman so early in his career.

'We need to talk,' she ordered, and marched back to the mobile café where the customers, still watching the small drama unfold, moved aside to let her buy two teas.

It was pointless claiming that he had no idea why the doctor should pick on him out of the blue, so the agent meekly followed and accepted the tea she thrust at him with an abrupt, 'No sugar. Your blood sugar levels are high enough.'

This was not the place to discuss MI5 secrets, within earshot of inquisitive gentlemen of the road, and the agent indicated they move to the cover of some bushes. 'So?'

Lottie took a long sip of tea which was surprisingly good considering it had been poured from a tarnished teapot constantly topped up all morning.

'I'm pretty sure that the security services of this country have more pressing things to do than follow me.'

'I can't discuss it.'

'Of course you can!' snapped Lottie. 'Because you

believe I'm the only one who can tell you what your masters need to know.'

He tried not to sound taken aback. 'So what do we need to know?'

'What caused a nuclear explosion in the middle of the English countryside on the eve of the Second World War.'

'So what caused it?'

'How the hell would I know? I'm a doctor, not a nuclear physicist. So there's little point in following me. The only people who could have told you that lived in Fairdamon.'

'And they are all dead.'

'So accept that this is one mystery which won't be solved, 007.'

'Don't you want to know how your father died, Dr Freeman?'

'Thought I did, Agent ..?'

The young man hesitated, and then offered, 'Call me Harrington.'

'Mr Harrington - why not. One name's as good as any other.' Lottie finished her tea and crushed the polystyrene cup. 'The more I discovered about that creep, I called father, the less it bothered me. If I do find out something of national importance I'll tell you, believe me.'

The agent had always suspected he had been sent on a wild goose chase by ageing superiors with a bee in their bonnet about the past. Being so young, it seemed like ancient history to him. So what if there had been this large explosion in a remote, old town; what had that got to do with the country's current problems? Lottie could tell that Agent Harrington believed his valuable time should have been spent tracking down more immediate threats, not bad-tempered doctors who resented it. There was nothing else for it but to give Lottie a deferential nod that admitted defeat, and leave under the bemused gaze of the lorry drivers who had been hoping for a little more action.

Chapter 52

There are personal mementos no other living soul should see. Everything Moses believed that the rest of the world needed to know about Fairdamon would be passed into the capable, if slightly bemused, care of Dr Duncan Parfait. Thankfully the man had a level-headed assistant to prevent the weight of the discovery overwhelming him, and partner who was a diver capable of distinguishing ruins from rocks. Between them they would ensure that the archaeologist remained totally sober when excavating the finds of the millennium. The prospect of more mercenary adventurers muscling in would have also been incentive enough to stop alcohol from passing his lips. Now it was time to immolate those precious memories that could not be shared.

The perfume of the midnight garden was soon overpowered by the smoke from the small bonfire Moses had lit. He gave a convulsive cough as the silk scarf he held to his nose failed to block out the fumes of the firelighter which helped the dry twigs burst into flame. The bonfire in a small circle of ground where Patsy had intended to plant an azalea was probably not doing much for the soil's ericaceous content, but the gardener would soon be compensated by holding total sway over her domain without the bother of a troublesome employer.

A full moon cast a silver sheen on the pile of photos and documents and fretted out the silhouette of the nearby shrubs like a decorative lattice.

Each precious record of an unusually contented life, despite its loss and isolation, met the fire and the ageing photos crackled a little before becoming nothing more than a brief incandescence.

Amongst them were photographic prints developed long before the rest of the world had discovered the properties of silver bromide. Was that really the image of Brother Petrus, the mediaeval chronicler who had resisted the temptation of betraying Fairdamon's secrets in his history? He looked surprisingly ordinary and slightly portly; the archetypal perception of a jolly friar with an element of Neville in his expression, which suggested he had been caught out in some futile good deed. How Moses would have liked to meet this man, extraordinary in his mediocrity. Brother Petrus had probably possessed a more profound understanding of Fairdamon philosophy than he did. This was no doubt why the monk had risked the charge of heresy to protect the ancestors of Moses from a vengeful church, and merely contented himself with a passing reference to "The Cult of Urial" in his great work, as well as the privilege of having his image graven onto strange paper without the intervention of human hands. That would indeed have been regarded as the work of the Devil by his superiors. He had also been wary of revealing the wealth of knowledge Fairdamons possessed about herbs, and persuaded his hosts to build a modest chapel where they could feign Christian devotion should their self-contained idyll ever be breached by rude human prejudice.

For all he learnt and saw in Fairdamon, Brother Petrus had remained a devout Christian, surprised that no one there had preached the virtues of Gnosticism to him. By the time he left the walled town he must have been sure they were committed to something much deeper and more profound. It was the only thing that could have accounted for the serenity of these enigmatic, golden people. No charitable soul, even the devout monk, had the right to question such spiritual maturity.

Moses took one last look at those rounded, amiable features, and then dropped the only image of a remarkable man into the flames. As the picture bubbled, Brother Petrus smiled a last goodbye.

Destroying the images of his father, brother, and mother was the most difficult. It felt like a betrayal, but nothing that could taint others by association must remain. He well remembered how the Secret Service had visited people the family had briefly befriended and was sure the Oradonte file still existed in a MI5 dossier. Some unsolved mysteries never died, especially those of nuclear explosions on the eve of World War II.

Night fell over the dying embers, leaving a pile of ash for Patsy to wonder over, as well as why the recluse had deserted his moss garden to sit where he would be overpowered by the moonlight fragrance of honeysuckle and rose.

Chapter 53

The next morning Moses opened the front door and beckoned in Duncan, Rolf, and Carol. He had expected the archaeologist to be alone but, by the sheepish expression the man wore, he had apparently been more overwhelmed at seeing the artefacts in the bank vault than Moses had anticipated.

'We had to come with him,' Carol explained, 'otherwise his brain might have exploded, and it's not easy to get stains like that out of the pillow.'

'It was becoming too much for the great man to shoulder by himself,' Rolf added. 'He is getting on after all.'

Duncan seemed too abashed to even acknowledge that his companions were gleefully making the most of his discomfort. Moses felt unexpectedly gratified that two strong personalities stood like sentinels on either side of an intellect which, at that moment at least, was not quite as resilient as he had calculated.

'Isn't your personal assistant here, then?' Duncan asked as they were led through the house and out of the French windows to the moss garden.

'Wendy is visiting her family in the Philippines to persuade them that the money she sends home has not originated from a house of ill repute or marriage of convenience.' Moses pointed back through the study. 'There is some freshly brewed coffee waiting in the kitchen. Just needs two more cups.'

'I'll do it.' Rolf knew that he was unlikely to miss anything important in the short time it would take and left to fetch the tray.

Moses invited Duncan and Carol to sit on the moss covered bank moulded like a settee. 'It is quite dry and will not stain.'

Carol trusted her cream trouser suit to the moss seat beside Duncan. Their host carefully lowered himself into his regular place to face them.

'How bad is it?' Carol asked without warning.

Duncan's jaw dropped: his partner had the habit of wading in where most men would quickly be out of their depth, not totally sure what she was referring to.

Moses knew all too well. 'Bad enough.'

'You need a doctor.'

'No,' Moses said firmly, despite the pain lining his face. 'I want no doctor to come near me.'

'You're suffering unnecessarily.'

Duncan shook his head to try and tell her to let it drop.

'There is a reason,' Moses explained patiently, 'but that is one secret which expires with me.'

Carol refused to believe any secret could be so terrible given how much he had already told Duncan, yet respected his wish to keep it. She opened her bag and took out a box containing ampoules of morphine.

'Carol...' Duncan began.

She ignored him. 'This is the best. From Switzerland, no doubt more potent than the stuff you've been getting locally.'

Duncan spread his hands in apology. 'I hardly said anything to the woman - I swear.'

Moses took the ampoules gratefully. 'Thank you. You must have run some risk to procure these?'

'Not as many as I would have liked. Couldn't push it. But they should last a couple of weeks until I can

160

get some more. Where do you keep the needles?'

Moses handed her a key from his waistcoat pocket. 'In the top drawer of the desk in the study.'

Carol took it and went back through the French windows.

'I'm sorry...' Duncan blustered.

'I am not. The last supply Wendy bought has almost gone. I was trying to ration it.'

'You should have let me know.'

'I would not dream of asking you to obtain drugs for me. Women seem to be much so much better at it anyway.'

Moses was right. Duncan would have been noticed immediately, even if he had dressed down and wore a sober suit. He would never be anything but disorganised, flamboyant, and that face people remembered from the TV.

As Rolf brought in their coffee he met Carol taking a small case from the drawer for their host.

'What goes on?' Rolf whispered as they went outside.

They were within earshot before she could answer so he put the tray on the moss table. 'Won't do any harm there will it?' he asked as a manuscript was nudged to one side.

'Not at all.' Moses took the case from Carol. 'Thank you.' He removed and ampoule to fill a hypodermic syringe then rolled up his sleeve and injected the morphine into his arm.

Carol placed a cushion she had also brought from the study to support his shoulders while it took effect. His features slowly relaxed as the fire in his chest was soothed.

'Any better?' she asked.

'Much. Thank you.' Moses turned to Rolf. 'So you are the remarkable young man who managed to work out the mystery no other academic would admit to?'

'I had these theories, but wasn't the only one,' Rolf admitted. He was intrigued. 'Just how right were they

161

then?'

'More than even you could imagine. My people evolved when the poles were at different latitudes and the continents of Antarctica and the Sahara Desert swarmed with life. We were here to see ice sheets grow and recede, the Earth sink in some places and push up mountains in others. We were here when the descendants of Homo erectus stood up on their hind legs and looked about them. No one but people as astute as you, Rolf, were willing to believe this of course. Yet, what are dreams to the level-headed often prove to be true - and I have the proof.'

Moses reached forward and picked up his translation of the ancient fragments. 'This contains our history. Much was destroyed by age or human hands, but many fragments were preserved by a mediaeval monk called Brother Petrus.'

Duncan respectfully took the document. 'Is this what you have been working on?'

'As best as I could. Some of the texts are so ancient I was unable to decipher them. Brother Petrus worked out a key and started the endeavour. Unfortunately he found he was translating events that could have had him branded as a heretic simply for reading about them, so stopped and returned them to Fairdamon. A librarian, Ko Tricali, continued the work until she died. For fear of it falling into the wrong hands, the council hid the fragments and took the translation no further. The box containing the original fragments is in the safe. I will let you have it before you leave.'

Carol felt the weight of the manuscript. 'Feels like a blockbuster.'

'There is a précis, which will initially be easier to digest. You should be the first to read it with your economist's eye. How our wealth was amassed would fascinate you.'

'Don't encourage her,' warned Duncan. 'She won't do my accounts if she gets sidetracked.'

Chapter 54

Duncan placed the box of fragments in his apartment's safe after being unable to make sense of the symbols, however much he studied them. He then settled down to read the précis of the translation wrestled away from Carol. It had been necessary to pull rank as the more qualified, and as a consequence condemn himself to fruitless hours with a spreadsheet and pocket calculator.

At the start of the document, Moses Oradonte had written a few pages in his immaculate hand on A4 to prepare the reader before they tackled the précis or full translation.

Fairdamon had existed before the Roman invasion as a refuge from the tribes its builders had unwittingly tried to help. Having succeeded all too well, these beneficiaries used their newly learnt metal technology to forge weapons instead of ploughshares. As soon as it became apparent that these warriors were more focussed on burglary than tilling the soil, the early Fairdamons had no choice but to protect their community with a high wall and sturdy bolts. The same thing had to be repeated by their kindred across the world who had encountered the same problem. Some tribes they had educated did settle down to farm and create prosperous cities before deciding that they wanted everyone else's prosperous cities. Greed seemed to be imprinted in the genes of these people. However dormant it had lain for centuries, it would inevitably rear up when temptation arose.

Once the wall had been installed around the town of Fairdamon these tall, mysterious strangers, having unwittingly generated mayhem, lived in self-sustaining isolation for centuries until the coming of the Normans. As the invader's agents were unable to gain entry to add an inventory of the town to the Doomsday Book, a considerable force was sent to impress on its residents that they were now William the Bastard's property.

If any records of the encounter were made, they no longer existed and no mention of Fairdamon and its population, its assets or arable land ever entered the Doomsday Book. What did survive were various myths about the town being populated by daemons that scattered the Norman army with thunderbolts. For centuries a local church displayed the charred chain mail and helmet of one of the accursed invaders. Villagers used to travel miles just to stand before it and pray for the same divine intervention on their behalf. Eventually an insecure lord of the manor ripped the mail from the wall and threw it in his moat.

It was a long while before the Church felt bold enough to investigate Fairdamon. Fear of thunderbolts still lurked at the back of authority's mind so the lowly, expendable, and fortunately open-minded, Brother Petrus was sent to stand before its impregnable walls and hope someone would feel enough sympathy for his poverty to allow him admittance.

Brother Petrus possessed more expertise in Latin than his superiors but, the worldly-wise, he also had the sense to remain menial so those superiors did not feel threatened by a greater intellect.

Like many a wandering friar, he enjoyed ale and a good meal, yet his quill remained his solitary mistress and stimulating conversation his only other indulgence. With an abbot striving to make his order a silent one, he could see the ability to reason going the same way as the charity his abbey used to be renowned for.

Fairdamon must have seemed an unlikely refuge from an existence hidebound by devotion, self-mortification and cult of martyrdom, yet he accepted his holy duty to infiltrate this congress of the Devil's own without question. Brother Petrus never did record how he was allowed in through the high walls which the Norman army had failed to breach. There was already enough magic attached to the town, and trying to explain it would have only generated more rumours. Fairdamons did sometimes leave their refuge to market their exquisite perfumes and exotic fruits which graced the tables of nobility. Thieves and authorities alike learnt to let the tall, distinctive strangers with frightening powers go about their business unhindered. Their protection also extended by association to the merchants and bankers who helped them amass fortunes great enough to bankroll the Crown.

Here the summary tantalisingly ended.

After learning its brief history, Duncan's first inclination was to visit Fairdamon. Moses Oradonte apparently had not intended him to do this as its location was not in the topographical information he supplied so he laid aside the précis to turn to the translation in copperplate handwriting on a silky, cream paper not found on the shelves of supermarkets.

Chapter 55

Lottie spent several days checking that she was no longer being followed. Yet she still took the precaution of hiring a car before driving by a circuitous route to the South Coast. Her MI5 shadow might have been aware that she had paid a call on the mother of a delinquent child there, and was hopefully too preoccupied with more important matters of national security to work out why. The world, even that corner inhabited by the Secret Service, was not ready to discover the truth about Moses Oradonte. This was one rare occasion when her doctor's instinct for medical revelation would have to be put on hold. What Lottie Freeman was about to do put the squalid treachery of her father into perspective, and she had to admit, thankfully, that they had little in common after all.

Night had fallen by the time she reached her

destination. An illuminated church tower clock hanging like a second full moon against the star filled sky guided her to the house with a wrought iron gate guarded by mythical beasts and front garden laid out like a chequerboard. Lottie sat in the car parked well away from the only street lamp in the cul-de-sac and contemplated the design for some while before it occurred to her that the limestone squares and bay trees represented a board game she was unfamiliar with. A couple of giants would need to make a couple of moves before she could fathom what the rules were.

The doctor became aware that she was subconsciously trying to find a distraction to delay committing an act that would daunt even her iron resolve.

There was no light in the topmost room. Meg had told Liz that Moses Oradonte's personal assistant must have been in the Philippines visiting her family and she had blurted it out with all the other useful gossip.

Lottie reached for her medical bag and silently left the car to walk in the shadows up to the house. The porch light was not on, though the path was faintly illuminated by the light shining through the stained glass of the front door. Everything was so quiet Lottie felt a chill of apprehension that this call had been left too late.

As she reached for the knocker the door gently opened under her touch.

In the hall there was no movement apart from distant, flickering candles reflected in a mirror.

Lottie quietly pulled the door to. Only after she had crossed the open plan hall and living room was it possible to see the moss garden filled with candlelight through the open French windows of the study.

Moses Oradonte was waiting there for her, watching the moon and stars like distant friends. Lottie silently joined him and placed her medical bag on the moss table. He was barely able to move, so she took a phial of morphine and needle from her case, rolled up his sleeve, and injected it. The pain had never been purged so swiftly before and generated a surge of relief verging on euphoria. The ability to use words returned and the fierce, ageing features of the first, and last, doctor Moses Oradonte would ever consult came into focus. Despite the description he had been given, Lottie Freeman was not what he had expected. But then, what should the daughter of the Nazi agent blown up by his people look like? He knew she held no resentment and, if anything, was endeavouring to suppress the sympathy she was aware that this patient would reject.

'What kept you?' Moses asked.

'I had a shadow. Unlike Peter Pan, I had to dispose of it before visiting Neverland.'

Moses waited patiently while she took his pulse, and then unbuttoned his waistcoat to listen to his heart with her stethoscope. It was in an odd position, but that was to be expected.

The condition of his lungs was more surprising. 'It's a wonder you can still breathe.'

'There is fire in every breath.'

'Does your assistant realise that you won't be here when she returns?'

'I want Wendy to come back to a quiet house and generous bequest. She, and Patsy, should not have to deal with the inconvenience of my death. That is what I pay a solicitor for.'

'So the affairs of your estate have been put in order?'

'They have been for some while. All that needs to happen now, is that I slip unobtrusively away.'

'Without an autopsy of course.'

'Under no circumstances must there be an autopsy.'

Moses straightened his back against the moss. There was an odd saintliness about the man on the verge of death and Lottie wished all her patients could have been so sanguine.

'I suppose you would like to know how your father

died?' he asked.

'I paid a visit to Fairdamon. I got the general idea.'

'What is it like now?'

'You've never seen it, have you?'

'Only in photographs. I wanted to visit it while I was still able, but could not afford to arouse suspicion.'

'Easily done that, believe me.' Lottie hesitated before asking, 'You never had children did you?'

'No.' Moses noted the relief in her expression. 'Even if it were possible, it would not have been wise.'

'Stupid question.'

'What is Fairdamon like?'

'Full of foxgloves, bracken, and ghosts.'

Moses smiled. 'Oh no. Any ghosts would not have been ours. Fairdamons believed in the ephemeral nature of this existence. What you know as death is to us reality.'

'There is also a bloody great hole where the central square used to be. I assume what was left of my father is at the bottom of it?'

'I have no doubt. A quick way to die.'

'Maybe, but I bet it came as one hell of a surprise.'

'Tell me, Dr Freeman, you see more death than most people, what do you believe?'

'We all go to heaven and suck oranges.'

'Honestly?'

Lottie saw no point in withholding her inner thoughts from a dying man. 'If we knew what happens to us after we die, there wouldn't be much point in us being here. If we could be certain it was Heaven, then we'd just lounge around doing nothing. If it's Hell, then no pharmaceutical company would be able to keep up with the demand for tranquillisers.'

'So?' Moses persisted.

'So, existence is probably nothing more than a state of mind. As the Good Book says, as you sow, so you shall reap - or something like that.'

'That is what we believe.'

Lottie paused. 'You don't say?'

'This tangible existence called reality is created by a person's intentions, perceptions and creativity.'

'You mean consciousness?'

'With our thoughts we make our world. My people believed that everything they made was the construction of their thoughts, and with their passing it would all dissolve back into the atoms it was formed from.'

Lottie imagined what it would be like to watch the deserted town of Fairdamon melt away into a quantum mist. 'What? Everything?'

'That is what I was taught.'

'You obviously don't believe it.'

'If I did, I would not have dedicated so much time to the last great venture a Fairdamon would ever make.'

'So you have entrusted the heritage of your species to a human?'

'A very trustworthy one, though a little overwhelmed at the moment.'

'I'm not surprised. Let me have his contact details in case he ever needs tranquillising.'

'His name is Dr Duncan Parfait.'

'Oh... Him.'

'His card it on my desk.'

'I doubt that one believes everything is a product of imagination.' Lottie was obviously beginning to find that thought oddly reassuring. 'As my brother's decadent grandson is wont to say, "cool".'

'Unfortunately, imagined or not, it hurts like hell, and I do not want to be here when the pain returns.'

'I dare not give you anything more powerful.'

'Of course you dare. That is why you are here. It is called necessary medication. It was our way of dealing with terminal pain. Unfortunately, there is no other Fairdamon I can depend on to administer it.'

He was right, but medical ethics insisted that Lottie ask first. It wasn't just a matter of the patient's consent; they had to insist. There was something disconcerting in the realisation that Moses Oradonte had been obliged to administer the fatal dose to his own mother. That alone would not excuse her from backing away now.

The doctor took an ampoule of insulin from her case and filled a syringe. 'How long has this condition existed in your people?'

'As long as there have been Homo sapiens. However much we tried to isolate ourselves, it returned with every new strain of influenza.'

'Of course, there wouldn't have been a large enough gene pool to build up resistance to them.'

'Indeed.'

'That is the problem with not being human.'

'How odd to hear a human say it.'

'So where did you come from? The stars, or an earlier species of hominid?'

'It was unlikely to be the former.'

'Pity our species weren't closely related enough to interbreed. We might have inherited better manners.'

'The die was cast long before humans evolved. Convergence meant that we eventually resembled each other, but in all else we might as well have been alien.'

As Moses' heart was on his right side, Lottie could only wonder at what other differences there were in his internal organs. Medical science would have been as astounded and baffled at an autopsy on a Fairdamon body as Duncan Parfait had been by their antediluvian treasure. All the more reason to ensure that Moses Oradonte was cremated. Lottie did briefly wonder whether she was right in denying humanity the knowledge of an earlier, hominid species. Fortunately the archaeologist would ensure that legacy was trumpeted throughout every media outlet. The doctor's only concern was to respect her patient's wishes and prevent the exploitation of his remains.

'I guarantee that heart failure will go on the death certificate. Are you ready?'

Moses looked up at the harvest moon illuminating the sky. 'Now would be a good time.' He took a card from his waistcoat pocket. 'Please phone my solicitor in the morning. She will make the necessary arrangements.'

Lottie accepted the card before selecting a vein deftly and injecting the fatal dose. 'You'll feel dizzy for a moment.'

'Thank you.'

'This feels wrong, even to me, and I've done it enough times.'

'Why?'

'Other hominids were regarded as brutish - look at the way we slander Neanderthals. Your people were more civilised than we will ever be, and intelligent enough to ensure no trace of their technology remained.'

Lottie could only imagine what her species would have done if they had laid hands on that. It was bad enough when they did work things out for themselves. At least it had been in her power to complete the one last act that would allow a remarkable species to dissolve into oblivion without human interference.

Ever the gentleman, Moses Oradonte closed his eyes to save anyone else the trouble and, with a barely perceptible sigh, passed away, reassured that cremation would ensure that no trace of his DNA remained.

Chapter 56

As Duncan Parfait read the translation he jotted down notes to plot out the draft for the most radical document since Martin Luther pinned his Denial of Indulgences to a Wittenberg church door. It took over a week. When he was satisfied, the archaeologist was taken aback at how his brief summary made the people who founded Fairdamon seem all the more remarkable. This would indeed deflate his reputation as a debunker of controversial theories.

Before he had chance to dictate the draft into electronic format Carol crept in and without warning snatched it from him and disappeared into to the lounge. Duncan didn't try to stop her. He was too tired to argue and curious to see her reaction.

Carol lounged back in her reclining chair and started to read the untidy, rounded handwriting:-

Life was different in those days. A time when primitive tribes lived in awe of the "golden giants" who traversed the skies in ships lifted by warm air, and sometimes arrived at their settlements to confer knowledge in their strange language. The giants were never threatening, only generous. These godlike visitors taught one tribe to spin thread from animal fur and plant fibres, another to grow crops and grind the seed to make flour.

Then the ice came. The knowledge of the golden giants enabled many to survive the centuries of unremitting winter and others to find their way to more temperate climates.

When the climate at last warmed living became easier by the lake margins and shores of the rising sea where food was plentiful. The memory of the golden giants faded after the barrier that held back the great ocean was breached and their glorious, gleaming cities were inundated. The steeples, ziggurats and domes submerged, the giants seemed to melt away from every part of the planet as though they had only been a mythical, magical dream.

They must have been gods. Perhaps they would return one day?

Tribal elders who survived into old age would relate tales of ancestors being shown glowing bowls filled with the sun and high-domed ceilings glittering with jewels that looked like the star filled night. These giants had a magic glass that, when pointed at the inky sky, conjured up globes banded with clouds, or flattened discs, and revealed the true, pockmarked face of the glowing creamy sphere that lit their tribe's way at night.

Once the daemons and their cities of crystal, gold and alabaster had gone, their knowledge was lost. Now, despite an increasingly benign climate, progress would be slow, bloody and bigoted. Those who did remember had no idea how many of the golden giants secretly survived. A legend claimed that they came from one of those dots sparkling in the night sky, others that they had been born from the breath of the volcano. Having erupted and laid waste to the world, this was the Earth's way of healing itself. The giants could not have been mortal because they had never been known to die, just fade from existence like the powdery snow blown from the tops of mountains.

But a small number did survive. Their technology had enabled these demigods to move into the cracks of a world now claimed by the descendants of the tribes they had saved from extinction. These ancient people had realised that, despite the efforts of their forebears to nurture them, the hominids would never change their nature. If the daemons did return, they would be seen as scapegoats for all the world's woes and not as benefactors.

While human civilisation expanded, despite the efforts of disease and disaster to purge the planet of the presumptuous creatures, the golden giants retreated to secret sanctuaries, only able to reproduce with their own kind. Eventually disabling anomalies meant that, one by one, their isolated populations succumbed to diseases they no longer had the power to control.

Carol lowered the summary and returned the owl-like gaze of Duncan who was standing over her. She was still struggling to believe such a world ever existed, though no longer willing to accuse him of becoming delusional.

Chapter 57

Wendy and Patsy stood in silence looking at the empty chair in the study.

Just before Moses Oradonte died, he had listed his bequests in folders neatly labelled with the intended beneficiaries and sealed them with gold wax before handing the documents to Miss Kandy. Even she found it difficult to resist opening them before the reading of his will, which dealt with his greater fortune divided between several charities, and a purpose built museum to display the Fairdamon treasure, and enough funding for Dr Duncan Parfait to excavate into his old age.

The handwritten bequests in the folder included instructions that his valuable volumes were to be donated to specialist libraries, the Art Nouveau, other collectables, fittings and furniture were to remain in the house for the benefit of its next owner, and the large grounds in which the mobile home of his faithful gardener sat became Patsy's.

Wendy was to inherit the house and its contents. It was necessary for Miss Kandy to repeat it several times before she would believe it.

Wendy was still trying to take in that she now owned the palatial property as she reverentially arranged the pens on Moses Oradonte's desk in the way he always did.

Patsy could tell that she was still overwhelmed. 'Your family could move here. The place is too big for one person.'

'The grandparents would like that,' Wendy murmured distractedly.

Patsy indicated the candles and joss sticks filling the moss garden with fumes powerful enough to make his ghost sneeze. 'He didn't intend you to turn it into a shrine, you know.'

'Mr Oradonte should not be forgotten, even though he was a private man who took with him many secrets.'

'Don't know what they were, do you?'

Wendy shook her head. 'I have no idea, and did not ask because it was unlikely he would have told me.'

It was obvious that Wendy had taken the loss of Moses hard, so Patsy tried to distract her. 'Anyone apart from your grandparents like to join you?'

'The rest of the family have lives in the Philippines, though my husband's parents have always wanted to leave since he was killed. They would be good company for my grandparents.'

'I suppose Miss Kandy could sort out the residents' permits.'

'As they have their own pensions, it should be possible.'

Wendy brightened a little at the thought and told Patsy with an unusually mischievous expression. 'Of course, we will depend on you to grow the produce they are used to.'

Patsy relished the challenge. 'You name it, I'll grow it. Rice paddy in the lower garden to collect the run-off from the cliff - no problem.'

She had no doubt that the gardener could do it. 'Though you will keep the moss garden, won't you?'

'Oh alright. Just one shrine.' Much to her embarrassment, Patsy had to brush away a tear. 'I'm going to miss that uptight, irritable man.'

Wendy knew what she meant. Unaccountably a gap had opened up in their lives as though some vital element had unravelled from the Universe, like a warp thread pulled from the fabric of existence. She did not believe in ghosts any more than Patsy yet, having lived in the same house for so long, she would always feel his presence.

There was a discreet knock at the distant front door, just loud enough to be heard in the silence that had descended.

Wendy automatically went to open it.

Standing on the doorstep was Moses' trim solicitor.

She was holding an urn.

Miss Kandy was a small, elegant young woman with the glowing honey complexion of a Bollywood star. Six inches taller and her ambitions could have taken a completely different turn. Moses Oradonte had just been relieved that his stunningly attractive legal adviser was unable to reach the top shelf in the supermarket. With discreet heels and sumptuously patterned shalwar kameez, she could weave in and out of the cracks of a complex business where even tall men in suits were barred entry, never perceived as a threat in this world of secrecy, solicitors and litigation.

Miss Kandy handed the ashes to Wendy. 'Are you sure you want to do this?'

Patsy joined them. 'Well he wouldn't have thanked us for scattering him over the pansies.'

Wendy led the way into the moss garden where she removed the lid of the green enamelled urn. She gently tipped it and the ashes of Moses Oradonte were caught by a light breeze which dusted the moss with a fine coating. They could almost feel the Earth sigh as it accepted them and, on cue, a light shower washed the mortal remains of a remarkable man into Nature's velvet, which had given him sanctuary from the noisy, nosy world outside.

The three women mourning his loss would never know that he was the last of a benevolent people who had guaranteed their own disappearance by saving humans from extinction.

'We should have had a service of some sort,' Patsy moaned.

'This was his way,' Wendy reassured her.

As the light shower stopped, Miss Kandy took a small box from her bag and opened it. 'This was found in his ashes.'

The two women peered at a tiny device glittering like a diamond.

'What is it?' asked Patsy.

'Mr Oradonte may not have known himself. No

mention of it was made in any of the papers relating to his will or estate.' The solicitor carefully lifted the small object in her immaculately manicured fingers. 'My instructions were to ensure that no trace of him remained, though it is difficult to see how this can be destroyed if it is capable of surviving a crematorium's furnace.'

'Probably a medical implant of some sort,' Patsy suggested. 'Perhaps that doctor knows?'

Miss Kandy looked surprised. 'You mean Dr Freeman?'

'Yes, I think that was her name.'

'Dr Lottie Freeman,' added Wendy.

The women gazed at each other for a brief moment and realised that they were all aware of the part that doctor had played in Moses Oradonte's final moments.

'She was the last, and probably only, doctor he ever saw.' The solicitor replaced the device and closed the box. 'I shall consult her as to its nature before taking further action.'

Patsy was impressed. 'Spoken like a true lawyer.'

Miss Kandy gave a disarmingly girlish smile. 'It is possibly of no importance.'

'I doubt that we shall ever know, along with all the other secrets he managed to keep.'

Chapter 58

Despite the haste with which Duncan Parfait had initially wanted to investigate the submerged sites on the map Moses had given him it was some while before he came to terms with his benefactor's death. A niggling thought was also trying to make him apprehensive about what would be uncovered. So, for several weeks Rolf became the driving force in organising the first excavation.

Eventually reality kicked in when Duncan realised its imperative when becoming aware of how determined Carol was to be the first to reach the ancient ruins. And then there was his ambition to shatter the convictions historians had lived with for centuries. The archaeologist knew he would never be forgiven - which made it even more tempting. It was his unlikely destiny to shoot down all those self-interested, self congratulatory preconceptions the human race had held about itself, especially the ones he had so smugly defended during his long career.

It was just as well Duncan Parfait had no idea of just how extraordinary Moses Oradonte had actually been. Lottie Freeman, for all her bombastic, crusading spirit, kept her word. The recollection of the only surviving member of a hominid species pre-dating her own dwindled into a rather quirky memory that would die with her - which didn't mean that the temptation to probe deeper totally disappeared. Lottie would have borrowed a bucket and trowel from her brother's shed to sally forth and illegally excavate Fairdamon herself, if only to annoy MI5. Knowing all too well she would make discoveries which would only complicate her - relatively - uneventful life, she decided not to. Yet there was a risk that the strange town would end up being investigated by the wrong people, so she sent a letter to Moses' solicitor asking her to recommend Duncan Parfait focus his attention on Fairdamon as soon as possible.

But there was one mischief Lottie simply couldn't resist - taking her sister-in-law through that breach in Fairdamon's high perimeter wall. She at least owed Maddie that much after tantalising the woman for so long.

It had to kept be secret of course. The mere mention of Fairdamon could catapult Fred into an uncharacteristic state of anxiety and neither of the women wanted him to have a stroke. Better he was left painting papier-mâché models for local good causes while they ostensibly took an outing to see the Eden project - or was it Kew Gardens? Once he lifted his paintbrush Fred was unable to recall which, and didn't even wonder at his strident sister's sudden interest in flowers.

By the hints dropped by Lottie, Maddie had the suspicion that she was being taken to a huge, secret garden and the machete she had brought along suggested it was somewhat overgrown. How overgrown she couldn't imagine until the two women eased past the wooden gate in Fairdamon's wall and looked down into an ancient valley where Nature had been free to let down her skirts and waft her pollen laden petticoats over the burgeoning meadows.

Fairdamon was the strangest place Maddie had ever set eyes on. The mere fact that it could only be accessed through a dilapidated gate hidden by briars and bracken explained Lottie's insistence she wear thick trousers and sturdy shoes. A warm Autumnal glow bathed the wild orchards and the mist evaporated from the dew-laden meadowland. The swifts and swallows nesting in overhanging eaves had left for Africa since Lottie's last visit, though the house martins still dipped and weaved over the ponds newly topped up by a recent cloudburst.

If anything, Fairdamon seemed even more magical.

Maddie now had a glimmer of why her sister-in-law had kept Fairdamon secret and the mere mention of it caused her husband's expression to freeze in apprehension.

As they descended into the town, Maddie resisted the urge to break off giant teasels and Chinese lanterns for flower arrangements. Lottie already regarded her handicraft interests frivolous and she did not want to confirm it by picking dead flowers whilst experiencing such a unique Italianate wonder.

They wandered through the ghostly streets to the deep crater where Lottie and Fred's father met his Valhalla. Maddie was confronted by the dilemma of whether to tell Fred to visit the town, or to leave him happily pottering around, making model ships and papier mâché figures for local children. But then, why disturb his retirement idyll by reminding him of that horrible episode from his family history? Lottie could revel in it enough for both of them, and Maddie had to admit that the brief adventure had punctuated the monotony of being married to her placid brother for over 50 years.

Chapter 59

As Duncan Parfait sat in the ship's observation room and examined the images appearing on the monitor from the remote camera, there could be no doubt that a remarkable city lay beneath the layers of silt. While Carol was on deck putting on her aqualung, his pulse raced at the prospect of uncovering it. Unmapped waters or not, she was going to be first diver down there with a camera.

The first images she sent back were of unusual, symmetrical rock formations. Closer examination revealed one of them to be an ornately carved archway of a domed building which had caved in after repeated earth tremors.

At that point Duncan had no choice but to summon her back so his team of professional archaeologists could take over. There was no way of telling what wonders - and hazards - lay beneath the immaculately worked sea-worn rubble of marble, granite, and obsidian. Given Carol's enthusiasm, Duncan was afraid some unstable column could collapse on her, and it soon became apparent that there were a lot of columns supporting precarious porticos, arches, roofs and bridges. In fact, the city was so vast there was a chance much of it would never be fully revealed.

Weeks of frantic activity followed, fascinating the inhabitants of the nearest harbour by its secrecy. At each new discovery, Duncan's first inclination was to tell Moses Oradonte; the fact that he was dead seemed oddly irrelevant.

At last the reality of what he and his team were doing sank in. For all the fame, fortune, prestige, and notoriety that awaited him, unaccountable misgivings entered the archaeologist's dreams at the very moment he should have been celebrating. Nothing about Moses had been simple and such a remarkable bequest could only come with a curse. He dismissed the irrational apprehensions. Unlike Rolf or Carol who would have known how to deal with them whatever the price fate demanded, he wasn't mature enough to pay up and get on with life. Not that Duncan had the time to let the haunted feeling slow down his enormous venture. There were many more sites to investigate before announcing to the world how deluded humankind had been about its own uniqueness.

The book was already half written: once Rolf had assembled all the chapters into a coherent manuscript and the results of the excavation were added, no publisher would dare turn it down. Only Carol was worldly-wise enough to understand the danger in snatching away the reassuring struts on which humanity had built up the image of its own self-importance. Her partner was hurtling headlong into a wall of outrage without so much as a comforting platitude to cushion the revelations. As he was by nature open and trusting, Duncan assumed the rest of the world to be reasonable.

Rolf also experienced some unease, but was reluctant to risk bringing his companion crashing to earth while he was on such a high. The young researcher's apprehensions were more difficult to make sense of. Although Rolf's meetings with Moses Oradonte had been fleeting, he had detected something unsettling and otherworldly about the man. Could their benefactor have bequeathed them more questions than answers?

Although they shared their misgivings, Rolf and Carol agreed to say nothing to Duncan. However realistic when it came to archaeology, he did believe in ghosts, and the last thing Carol wanted was him to do was to start checking under the bed before putting out the light.

Chapter 60

After her encounter with Moses Oradonte, Lottie found life's other trials and tribulations something of an anti-climax. She wasn't even surprised when Miss Kandy personally delivered the small device picked from his ashes. The doctor had no idea what it was either, so it sat on her desk in its open box, a bright pinpoint of distraction when diagnosing patients and listening to their woes. Over the weeks it appeared to grow dimmer, which she put down to the days getting shorter and her need for new glasses.

One morning, before the lights went on in her consulting room, the device was barely visible. At first it had sparkled in daylight, now the life had left the small crystal like Tinkerbell's light going out.

With a jolt, Lottie recalled one of the last things Moses had told her. Before meeting him she would have not believed it - now anything seemed possible.

Lottie scrabbled through drawers and piles of medical records before finding the notebook in which she had jotted down Duncan Parfait's landline number. She didn't know why Miss Kandy had given it to her, though subconsciously she might have anticipated that something like this would happen.

Hand shaking, she dialled, praying it wouldn't be picked up by an asinine message on an answerphone.

Thankfully there was a woman's voice, 'Hi, this is the residence of Calamity Clara and Munching Munchkin.'

Asinine the cultured voice may have sounded, but at least it was human.

'This is Dr Lottie Freeman.'

Carol's tone immediately became professional. 'I know that name.'

'I signed the death certificate of Moses Oradonte.'

'Rolf's team aren't asking you to prescribe them tranquillisers, are they?'

'You'll need a ton of them if what Mr Oradonte told me is true.'

Carol had been anticipating the fly that would drop into the ointment of Duncan's great adventure, but hadn't expected it to be tossed there by a doctor. 'I don't think I want to hear this.'

'Are you monitoring the undersea excavation?'

'Got a video link set up.'

'Look at it.'

Like most people unable to resist an order from the doctor's tone, Carol went to her laptop and logged on to the underwater camera link. The image was clear now that the Mediterranean waters had settled from the last excavation and the city ruins could be distinctly seen.

'What am I looking at?'

'Hopefully only what you expect to see.'

'Do I say something to the great man?'

'No. Just hope I'm wrong.'

'Wrong about what?'

'Keep watching.' Lottie placed the box containing the device in the darkness of a drawer to totally shield it from the light. She held her breath as the last photon left it. The implant Moses Oradonte had unknowingly carried inside his body for so long was now totally dead. 'If anything is going to happen, it should be about now.'

Carol's apprehension mounted when the undersea camera was buffeted by a freak current. 'Something's happening.'

The huge, ancient ruins were beginning to dissolve.

There was no Alka-Seltzer fizz or turbulence to suggest an external agent was responsible. The monolithic masonry was just merging with silt and water.

Lottie heard a disbelieving catch in Carol's voice. 'That's not possible...'

The doctor tried to keep a detached sympathy in her tone, even though she could understand what was going through her mind. 'Moses Oradonte told me his people had an ancient belief that everything they created would dissolve when t**he last Fairdamon** died.'

'This will destroy Duncan.'

'Where is he?'

'Working on the book in the British library, so I can't phone him. Do you think this is happening at all the sites that haven't been excavated?'

'Quite likely. Even Moses Oradonte didn't believe it possible.'

'But why?'

'His people were more remarkable than we can ever imagine - even he could imagine.'

'I don't understand.'

'With their thoughts they made their world.'

Neither of the women believed in magic, so assumed it had to be some mysterious quantum effect. The Fairdamons' comprehension of matter and consciousness must have been far in advance of human understanding. Their physicists had spent millennia contemplating them after all. How else could their existence become part of a quantum anomaly? The economist was glad she had decided against becoming a scientist: the ones she knew would have lost their reason, watching matter dissolve before them.

Carol barely heard Lottie saying, 'Sorry...' before lowering the phone to watch the columns, walls, and archways she had spent so much time exploring being absorbed back into the sea floor, leaving hardly an indentation.

When she was able to collect her thoughts, she pulled out the folder filled with printouts of the underwater excavation. Thankfully the images were still there. Though when the safe door was opened, all that was left of the ancient fragments inside the box Moses had given Duncan was a pile of dust. Only his translation and the antique spectacles of Ko Tricali remained.

A cold tickle of trepidation skittered up Carol's spine. A rationalist to the last, this was too inexplicable to reason away. Matter did not dissolve, disintegrate, or disappear without good scientific cause. Whatever quantum aberration was at play here no physicist she had encountered would have dared explain it, let alone admit that it could happen.

Despite being strong I can minded, Carol could not decide what to do next. Should she leave a text message for Duncan or, preferably, contact Rolf to break the devastating news or even one of those physicists to arm her with a plausible sounding explanation to try and prevent her partner plunging into permanent melancholia?

For all the ancient artefacts Duncan and his team had excavated, their catalogue was useless without the real articles as proof. Carol could visualise him going down in history as a delusional fantasist who used CGI and PhotoShop to prove his argument. How could he be expected to part with the dream that Moses Oradonte had, in all innocence, offered him. It was unlikely the realists on his excavation team would risk losing their reputations by backing him up. The unenviable task of easing Duncan back into the real world - whatever that was - would fall to Carol.

Chapter 61

Moses' solicitor and his bank manager stood gazing in amazement at the treasure in the Oradonte vault.

Miss Kandy took out her spectacles.

No, she had not been mistaken. The busy mist surrounding some of the artefacts was real enough. Molecules were evaporating from the precious objects like sunlight hitting frost.

Could any relic be so ancient that it would eventually dissolve unless kept in a vacuum? There was nothing in Moses Oradonte's comprehensive papers to explain this. He had even set aside a fortune for the Fairdamon hoard to be housed in a purpose-built museum.

Could the ancient treasure have been stored in the wrong environment? As soon as the change in humidity had been detected by the vault's sensors, solicitor and bank manager immediately thought that - then dismissed the idea. Despite having outlooks that did not accommodate the irrational, they doubted that there was a scientific explanation for what they were seeing.

The delicacy with which a fluted vase was transformed into a spiral of smoke, making a bizarre pattern which suggested that there were fairies at work here. Then there was a sudden 'pop' when the shell of a sealed container cracked and the ancient air pressure inside it equated with the bank vault's. As the ornament shattered it became a halo, shimmering like a ring round and invisible Moon before dissipating.

Soon, the less substantial relics had all but disappeared, leaving blossoms of pearlised clouds that merged into the harsh, fluorescent light.

'You do know we are breathing this stuff in, don't you?' the bank manager observed.

Miss Kandy could not believe, deep down in her soul, that her late client would have bequeathed anything harmful to an unsuspecting world. He did have secrets he would not share with his legal adviser, but she believed that there were good reasons for it and that none of them was mendacious.

'I know, but I'd sooner be in here than outside breathing traffic fumes.'

As though suddenly remembering that she was a legal practitioner, the solicitor took out her smartphone to record that this was actually happening. 'This is being recorded on your security cameras, isn't it?'

'Oh yes, as soon as we noticed something odd when the humidity levels became erratic.'

Miss Kandy continued to record the disintegration of the artefacts until the phone's memory was exhausted. She had to have something to show Moses' executor who, until then, been happy to accept that the hoard of treasure existed on paper. He at least had the right to see what he had missed.

'I realise that these artefacts must be ancient, but what are the chances of them disintegrating all at once?' asked the bank manager.

'I'm no chemist, but very little I should think.'

He was still puzzled. 'You don't sound too appalled? Our insurance is unlikely to cover this. Fire, flood, act of God... What category does this fall into for goodness sake?'

'This is just history. Most of the estate is locked up in bonds and gold.'

Yes, he thought, priceless history which he thankfully wouldn't be held to account for losing.

The two of them remained watching, mesmerised as precious minerals slowly atomised and were reduced to plumes of precious dust. It was pointless calling in experts to try and conserve them. By the time the right specialists were found the vault was unlikely to even contain traces of the chemical elements the artefacts had been crafted from.

As the heavier objects dissipated, dissolving in blooms of mist like water jets hitting bath foam, bubbles of molecules broke away and floated over the heads of the observers before popping out of existence in a rainbow shimmer.

Gold vaporised in glowing halos and ancient alabaster figurines became crazed with fine cracks before turning to powder from the inside out, leaving the shells to gently implode. Crystalware, amber, carnelian, and jade all melted away in the colours

187

peculiar to the elements they had been formed from.

Despite the bank manager's warning, Miss Kandy reached out to touch the dissolving material.

It had no heat.

In their small watchroom, the bank's security team, joined by two under managers, watched and recorded, too astounded to make assumptions about what was happening.

Eventually, all that remained were small piles of powder reverting to their crystalline elements.

Miss Kandy replaced her smartphone. 'My client's vault now appears to be no longer needed. Can you have the final account drawn up?'

The bank manager said nothing.

He needed a stiff drink.

Chapter 62

Lottie had no idea what induced her to call MI5 and tell Agent Harrington to rendezvous at Fairdamon.

By the time she arrived and had scrambled through the bracken, brambles and gate in its wall, the ghostly town was already crumbling like an exotic sandcastle in a slowly swirling vortex.

She found the MI5 agent standing at the head of the path, looking down into the valley, his long raincoat flapping in the breeze as though he had just stepped from Wuthering Heights.

'Who told you how to contact me?' he asked without turning to look at her.

'The same way you knew I was standing behind you.' Lottie obviously wasn't going to admit that she knew someone who could hack into the personnel files of the Secret Service. MI5 were well aware people did it just because they could: the most adept were usually recruited into computer security and the less able found that their hard drives had been mysteriously wiped. Given what was happening below them at that moment, national security seemed irrelevant. In the face of ancient magic of this magnitude. There was no sensible explanation for the disintegration of the buildings, some of which must have been standing since the Middle Ages.

'Why aren't you recording this?' asked Lottie.

'For the same reason you aren't.'

'What's that?'

'Because neither of us is here. Neither of us ever was.'

The young man had a point. As she grew older, the last thing the doctor wanted was life to become too interesting, and the agent needed an interrogation about what he had been doing there even less. With no more Fairdamon to clog up MI5's already overstretched workload, it could now hopefully dwindle into the historical files and rot away before some sad soul with nothing better to do decided to scan everything into electronic format.

Until that day, Agent Harrington had been a reasonably well-balanced, diligent soul. The opportunity to be anything else had never presented itself during his privileged upbringing. In one brief phone call, Dr Lottie Freeman had changed all that. Now, for the sake of his sanity, he would be obliged to join that elite collection of witnesses who would never be believed if they admitted what they had seen. The only way to save the peace of mind of others, was at the expense of his own.

'Is there any admission fee to this club you have tricked me into joining?'

Lottie had been so engrossed by the spectacle of the tumbling masonry, windmills, and marble columns she didn't register what he had asked at first. 'Club?'

'You know damn well anyone aware that this is happening will have to keep their mouths shut. We might as well all be in a club, like derided UFO spotters. We can't even have it printed on a T-shirt.'

'Don't worry about it. I can prescribe something to

calm you down if you start experiencing palpitations in the middle of the night.'

'Thanks,' he replied, gratitude the last thing on his mind.

Doctor and agent then stood silently as the remnants of Fairdamon gently tumbled into discrete mounds amongst the overgrown orchards and irrigation runnels.

Agent Harrington eventually turned to face Lottie, 'So, what was that all about?'

'Quantum anomaly.'

'Bullshit.'

'Depends in which dimension the bull evacuates its bowels.'

'You are seriously telling me that these people had never been real?'

Lottie thought about it. 'It's more likely that we are the ones with only one foot in reality.' She paused. 'You're really not going to report this, are you?'

'Just why did you bring me here?'

'I suppose it was as a witness to a closure for a people who deserve to rest in peace,' Lottie admitted.

The agent gave a snort of contempt to conceal how perplexed he was.

'They are all dead now, you know,' Lottie assured him. 'You can relax because there is nothing left for you to investigate, if that is what bothers you. But if it does ever get out, leave it to the conspiracy theorists of the future to fathom. By the time the file on Fairdamon can be made public, humans might have comprehended how it could all happen.'

'You don't know, of course?'

'I only know the legend.'

'What legend?'

'When the last Fairdamon dies, everything they created will disappear.'

'Why, for goodness sake? Other people have become extinct, but at least they left ruins.'

'The human brain hasn't yet developed the capacity

to comprehend existence.'

'And these Fairdamons had?'

'Quite probably.'

'So that means they weren't human.'

It was an ironic observation, but Lottie's silence spoke volumes.

Agent Harrington fixed his gaze on a point in the distance and he shuddered. 'You have to be kidding?'

There was no reply.

Lottie Freeman turned and walked back to her car, leaving the young man standing like a romantic poet seeing the Alps for the first time.

He continued to stare at the place where Fairdamon once stood, ignoring his mobile and the drops of rain that were developing into a heavy shower.

He stood there until the rain stopped, the wind nudging him back to his own dimension. Then a whisper chilled his soul, 'Reality is illusion, only thoughts make your world...'

THE END